MW00808043

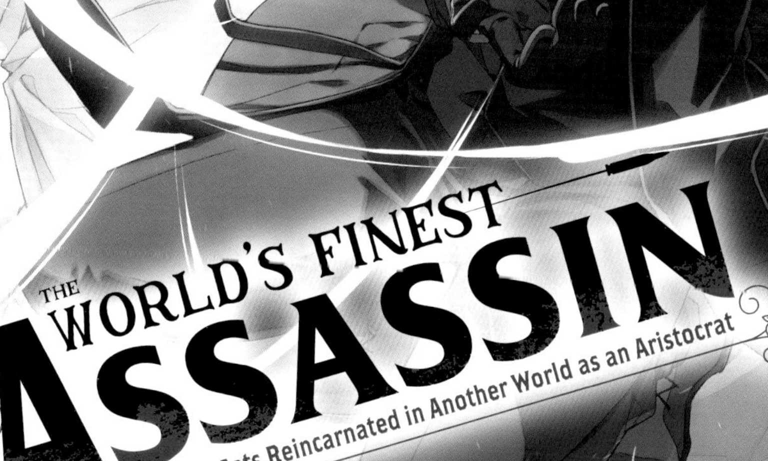
THE WORLD'S FINEST ASSASSIN
Gets Reincarnated in Another World as an Aristocrat

Contents

The World's Finest Assassin Gets Reincarnated in Another World as an Aristocrat

† Goddess
A system designed to protect the world.
† Dia
Circumstances led to her becoming Lugh's little sister. She is among the strongest mages in the world.

"Yes, it's been
a long time.
I was so lonely
without you."

† Tarte
Lugh's personal retainer and his assassination assistant. She cares deeply for Lugh because he saved her life.
† Nevan
A daughter of one of the four major dukedoms. She represents the peak of humanity.
† Maha
The proxy representative of Lugh's cosmetics brand. She provides logistical support by collecting funds, information, and more.
† Lugh
The oldest son of the clan of assassins, who is often called a boy genius. He was the world's greatest assassin in his previous life, and he combines that knowledge with the magic of his new world.

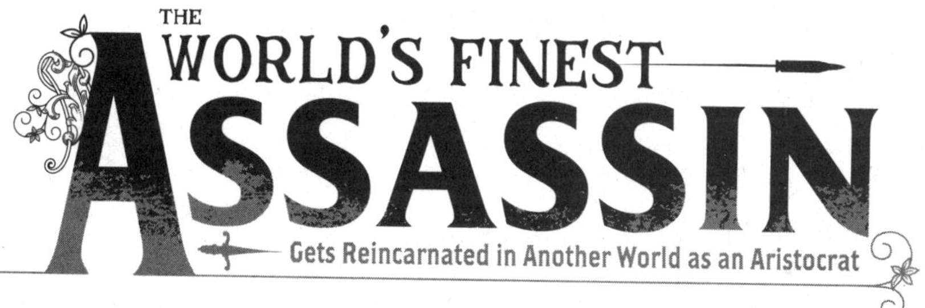

5

Rui Tsukiyo

Illustration by Reia

New York

The World's Finest Assassin Gets Reincarnated in Another World as an Aristocrat, Vol. 5
Rui Tsukiyo

Translation by Luke Hutton
Cover art by Reia

Yen On
150 West 30th Street, 19th Floor
New York, NY 10001

Visit us at yenpress.com
facebook.com/yenpress
twitter.com/yenpress
yenpress.tumblr.com
instagram.com/yenpress

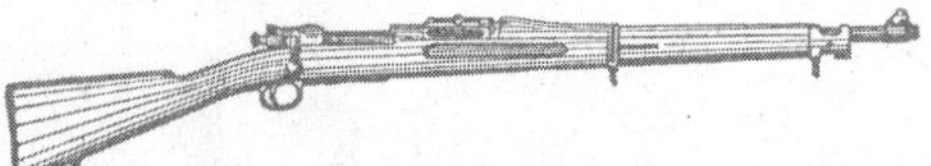

First Yen On Edition: June 2022
Edited by Yen On Editorial: Jordan Blanco
Designed by Yen Press Design: Andy Swist

Yen On is an imprint of Yen Press, LLC.
The Yen On name and logo are trademarks of Yen Press, LLC.

Library of Congress Cataloging-in-Publication Data
Names: Tsukiyo, Rui, author. | Reia, 1990- illustrator.
Title: The world's finest assassin gets reincarnated in another world / Rui Tsukiyo ; illustration by Reia.
Other titles: Sekai saikou no ansatsusha, isekai kizoku ni tensei suru. English
Description: First Yen On edition. | New York : Yen On, 2020–
Identifiers: LCCN 2020043584 | ISBN 9781975312411 (v. 1 ; trade paperback) | ISBN 9781975312435 (v. 2 ; trade paperback) | ISBN 9781975333355 (v. 3 ; trade paperback) | ISBN 9781975334574 (v. 4 ; trade paperback) | ISBN 9781975334659 (v. 5 ; trade paperback)
Subjects: LCSH: Assassins—Fiction. | GSAFD: Fantasy fiction.
Classification: LCC PL876.S858 S4513 2020 | DDC 895.6/36—dc23
LC record available at https://lccn.loc.gov/2020043584

ISBNs: 978-1-9753-3465-9 (paperback)
978-1-9753-3466-6 (ebook)

10 9 8 7 6 5 4 3 2 1

LSC-C

Printed in the United States of America

Prologue | The Assassin Brings Home a Guest

We had defeated the demon Liogel and parted ways with Naoise, who had been tainted by darkness. Although things seemed bleak, I trusted that I would reconcile with Naoise, and I was determined to save him from the path he'd started down.

Afterward, I drew up files outlining the gist of our victory over Liogel while excluding Naoise's involvement and entrusted them to Nevan's subordinates. The retainers were extremely skilled, and I knew they would be able to handle it. I expected they would supplement the report where necessary before submitting it to the kingdom.

"Wow, the wind feels so good!" Dia exclaimed, her eyes shining as she held down her fluttering hair.

We were gliding through the sky using a hang glider I'd produced with earth magic, and I was using wind magic for course correction and acceleration. Our destination was the Tuatha Dé domain.

This glider could support two people. I was piloting it, and Dia was my firmly secured passenger. We were greatly enjoying our trip through the air.

Hang gliders were an effective method of travel that didn't consume much mana. Previously, I'd considered conjuring a vehicle like a car or a motorcycle. Given my knowledge and magic capabilities, it should have been doable.

The issue was the lack of paved roads on which to comfortably drive, which meant I wouldn't be able to get the best use out of them. Thus, I settled on a hang glider.

It wasn't just convenient; soaring also felt fantastic.

"Oh, I'm so jealous. I wish I had gotten to ride with Sir Lugh, too."

"Lady Nevan, please don't remind me. You're making me sad."

I heard Nevan's and Tarte's voices through the communication device I had attached to my ear.

I had produced two hang gliders. Tarte was piloting the other one, and Nevan was her passenger. A hang glider for four people would have been huge and less aerodynamic, so I'd elected to make a pair of two-person ones.

I could have created a giant wind cowling to carry four people like I did the other day, but that method of travel consumed too much mana and wasn't fit for long-distance flights.

Tarte and I were the wind magic users of the group, so I controlled one and she the other. I took Dia as my passenger, and she had Nevan.

"I'm impressed you mastered flying so quickly, Tarte," I observed.

"It's surprisingly easy!" she replied.

"I would love to try flying it, too," added Nevan.

"Really? You can try once we get back to Tuatha Dé. You can't fly without wind magic, but you could still enjoy gliding."

"That sounds wonderful!"

"Hey, don't forget me. I want to fly one, too! There also must be a way to gain speed without wind. All you need is propulsion," said Dia.

"Dia, I really hope you're not thinking of using an explosive spell," I remarked.

Dia's two elemental affinities were earth and fire, so the easiest way for her to achieve propulsion would be via some kind of rupture. The force would be sufficient to fly, but the hang glider itself would not survive.

"Ah-ha-ha-ha, of course not. I have a better idea!"

"Make sure to tell me about it beforehand. You're scaring me a bit."

"Roger that, Lugh. My idea does involve science and physics, so I'd be uneasy about it without consulting you anyway."

Dia was a genius. Knowing her, she'd be able to use magic to create something resembling a jet engine.

"That's not good. The weather's getting rough," I observed.

My hang glider began to sway. The wind was growing more turbulent, and its direction was becoming erratic.

"Doing okay, Tarte?" I asked.

"Yes. It's a little scary, but I can manage. I will call for help if anything happens," she answered.

"Please do."

A straight flight was one thing, but I was worried at the thought of her having to fly through inclement weather.

"These communication devices are so useful, Sir Lugh. Did you make these with magic, too?" inquired Nevan.

We were able to speak over the distance between our hang gliders thanks to some radio earpieces I'd built. There was no way we would have been able to hear each other while soaring through the sky without them.

"While they use magic, they're a product of science."

All you needed to develop a radio communication device was a junior-high-level knowledge of physics. If you could also use earth magic to produce materials and manufacture them with a high degree of precision like me, they would be simple to make.

The radios were not without a few limitations, however. Because of their portable size, their range of communication was only about one hundred meters. I would have to make improvements later.

Despite the current issues, the tools would already be hugely advantageous in this world, which still relied on primitive methods of communication.

Quickly delivering information was difficult here. Consider the military, for example. It used messengers to run and convey things during operations. The accuracy of the reports was often low because of the game of telephone performed by the various recipients. What's more, there was a delay before any news arrived, and the situation could change entirely in the meantime. There was no guarantee the messenger would so much as arrive safely, and an enemy might steal the information.

Radio communication was massively advantageous by comparison. Orders and updates could be handed out safely and in real time. The difference in speed and accuracy would allow any army to overcome a massive strength disadvantage.

Radio communication promised to single-handedly change war forever.

"Science is truly astounding. I am regretting my promise more and more. This alone would allow humanity to take another step forward."

As I'd expected, Nevan took a great interest in wireless transmitting.

Nevan had made a promise not to misappropriate the knowledge and technology she gained from traveling with me. She understood the value radio communication would have in military matters as well as mercantile ones. She knew it could upset the present balance of the world, and that must have been vexing for her.

"I can't have this revealed to the public… I'm sharing it with you because I trust you. I would rather you not forget that," I warned.

"Have no fear. I still want to spend my life with you, Sir Lugh. I would never do anything to upset you," Nevan assured me.

Hearing her say things like that was both embarrassing and terrifying. I did trust her to an extent, though. Otherwise, I wouldn't have revealed radio communication to her in a non-emergency scenario.

"Tarte, watch out. Heavy wind incoming!"

"Okay. Whoa, that is strong."

An enormous gust buffeted us from the side. The wings of my hang glider creaked and then lost their balance, causing us to fall into a tailspin. I knew the wings weren't going to break because I had constructed them to bend and dissipate force in a situation like this.

However, that was what sent us into the plunge.

"AAAAAH!" screamed Dia.

Undoubtedly, this was frightening for her.

The worst thing about a tailspin was the panic that came from not knowing which way was up. Because we were at a reasonable altitude, my best option was to wait for the wind to calm down and restore balance once I got a grasp on the predicament. Anyone in their right mind would realize that.

However, distress causes one to act without thinking.

Once I got our tailspin under control, I checked above and below. I oriented the hang glider accordingly and started to glide again.

I searched for Tarte and found her ahead of us. She had made all the right moves without getting flustered.

"Impressive."

I was surprised by how coolly she'd handled the incident despite this being her first flight.

Tarte compensated for her lack of natural intelligence with hard work. She didn't mind forming countermeasures ahead of time for all imaginable situations, which made her highly reliable.

However, her ability to adapt was poor. She was not quick-witted when dealing with the unexpected. It was a weakness of hers.

Despite that, Tarte had dealt splendidly with a sudden difficulty. All of her hard work had likely built a strong foundation within her. She had persevered in her training to gain a great many skills, and it had increased her underlying strength.

She had truly grown. I decided I would rely on her more from now on.

Tarte and I used wind magic to quickly lift ourselves from our lowered altitude.

"You handled that well."

"It was all thanks to your training, my lord!"

That made me happy to hear.

"At this pace, we'll reach Tuatha Dé in no time. Hang in there."

"Yes, my lord."

I figured she'd had enough practice by now. I used wind magic to accelerate past her, then signaled for her to follow. We were moving significantly faster than before.

This was a practical assessment for Tarte. Given her current skill, I was sure she could handle this speed just fine, though.

We landed the two hang gliders in the courtyard at the estate.

"Flying through the sky really does feel incredible! I could get addicted to that," said Dia.

"I'm a little tired, but it was fun," Tarte agreed.

"Hang gliders are such an incredible invention. They're so

fast, and they can soar above enemies... I can think of so many applications for them. And that's not to mention radio. Oh, how I wish I could use all these treasures right in front of my eyes."

I pretended not to notice Nevan's grumbling as I stretched to loosen up my stiff body, then stepped into the estate. I heard footsteps race toward us.

"Welcome home, my adorable little Lugh! I've been waiting for you to get back. We can't throw the party without you."

"Hello, Mom."

Despite being around forty, she looked so young that she could have passed for being in her teens.

Mom hugged me, and her eyes went wide when she saw the girls behind me.

"Oh my, you've brought home another wife, Lugh."

"Dia and Tarte are not my wives, and I don't have that kind of relationship with Nevan," I retorted.

"Really?" Mom asked, tilting her head.

Nevan approached her.

"It is a pleasure to meet you. I am Nevan Romalung. I plan to marry Lugh and bring him into my household someday. I look forward to getting to know you, *Mother.*"

Nevan gave an elegant bow in the noble style. It was so graceful that it made me sick.

Dia and Tarte stiffened at her bold declaration.

Mom looked unusually serious.

"Do you mean *the* Romalungs?" she asked.

"Yes, *the* Romalungs," Nevan replied.

My mother avoided going to aristocratic gatherings, but she was a baron's wife. House Tuatha Dé and House Romalung had an inseparable relationship. As such, she recognized the name, as well as the family's true nature and its secret role in the kingdom.

"This is a surprise. You have it rough, Lugh. Being this popular can't be easy. But I can't approve of you marrying into her family. You can't leave me. I'll cry if you move away."

"I have no plans to wed Nevan, let alone move into the Romalung estate," I offered, but somehow, it seemed like neither one of them heard me.

"If you cannot stand to be apart from him, you are welcome to move in, too, Lady Esri. I promise you will know our best hospitality."

"Hmm-hmm, that is not an option. I am a Tuatha Dé woman."

My mother and Nevan both laughed. Something told me I needed to do something to defuse the tension.

"Anyway, I invited Nevan here as a guest. What was that about a party, Mom?" I asked.

I decided the best thing to do would be to change the subject. That wasn't a permanent solution, but it would give me time to think of something.

"Ah, I've been so excited to tell you. You're going to be an older brother, Lugh!"

"...Are you saying you're pregnant?"

"Yes! I have a feeling it's a little sister. My instincts are usually right. I would like you to give me a name for her, Lugh."

"O-okay, I'll think about it."

"Hmm-hmm, you don't need to worry about it that much. Whatever you choose will be fine."

I was taken aback by this sudden development. I wasn't sure if I should be happy or concerned.

"Tarte, Dia, if you two have children, I'll raise them together with my daughter. Wouldn't it be wonderful if Lugh's little sister and his children grew up like siblings?" my mother said.

"That sounds nice. I'm nervous about raising my firstborn anyway," answered Dia.

"U-um, I had a lot of siblings, so I can help!" offered Tarte.

My mom had been joking, but Dia and Tarte were totally on board with the notion. I watched in disbelief as the idea gradually took shape.

Also, it was apparent that my mother refused to call Nevan by her name. She must have really hated the idea of me being married off.

Nevan was puffing up her cheeks with frustration, but I knew that was an act to garner attention.

"I'm not planning on having any children right now," I stated.

It was customary in this world for nobles my age to have offspring. I didn't want to do anything to decrease my fighting strength until after the hero problem was resolved, though, and I hoped to enjoy some more time dating before becoming a parent.

"That's a shame. Anyway, come on in. I'm sure you all are tired, so I'll make something good for digestion. Consider it an appetizer for the all-out feast I'm preparing for tomorrow's celebration. Lugh, Tarte, I'd appreciate your assistance with that." My mother smiled at the two of us.

I gave her a nod. "That's fine with me. I'll take care of the hunting. I haven't had Alvanian rabbit in forever."

"Me too," Tarte added. "I'll pitch in with the food."

There'd been a major surprise waiting for me, but it felt nice to be home all the same. I was looking forward to a bit of rest and celebrating my new family member.

It was time to go to the forest and secure some food for the feast.

Chapter 1 | The Assassin Tests an Improved Spell

Not long after returning home, I left to go hunting. I was stalking deep in the woods to keep from disturbing the hunting ground the citizens of the domain frequented.

"A little sister… Gaining a new family member doesn't sound so bad."

I was shocked at first, but that had since given way to excitement.

It also meant I could not allow myself to die. So long as I was a Tuatha Dé, my sister would be able to live as a typical noble. Yet if I died, she would inherit the clan, meaning she would have to become the blade of the kingdom.

I didn't want that to happen. I wanted my sibling to live a regular existence.

That was what I thought about as I hunted.

I was also testing out a remodeled version of my wind probing magic.

"Found one. This new version is useful. I can tell the forest is especially lush and fertile this year. Dia will be happy to have Alvanian rabbit."

I had a fondness for the spell that allowed me to search my surroundings by merging my consciousness with the wind to broaden my area of perception. I used it quite often.

This was an improved version of that. Until now, the variant I had employed expanded outward as a circle with me as the starting point. As the range grew wider, it became more burdensome to maintain.

It's easy to understand if you imagine a circle. Assume I enlarged the area of my search to one meter. The scope of a circle with a radius of one meter is about three square meters, and the size of one with a radius of two meters is about twelve square meters. That's only an increase of nine square meters.

However, if I were to expand my search area from a circle with a radius of 100 meters to a circle with a radius of 101 meters, the field would increase by 631 square meters. This problem limited the coverage of my search.

Thus, I devised a remodeled version with a new formula.

This new iteration didn't scan an entire circle at once; it just extended a long rectangle some dozens of centimeters wide in front of me. I could only see what was ahead, but if I rotated the rectangle around myself, I could map out everything in all directions. I detected everything at a fraction of the cost, and the burden wouldn't grow exponentially every time I increased the range.

By nature, it was pretty similar to radar, and was very effective.

There is one big weakness, though.

Because I was rotating a rectangle, I didn't sense the entire area at all times as I had before. The time required to turn the scanning zone a full circle was less than 0.1 seconds, but oversights could still happen. Usually, that wouldn't be a problem, but it could prove fatal in a highly mobile or close-combat scenario.

For that reason, I needed to swap which method I selected depending on the situation. I would use the circular version when 0.1 seconds could prove fatal and the rectangular one at all other times.

All right, time to start hunting.

I produced a crossbow from the Leather Crane Bag I used to store objects in an alternate space. Guns possessed greater range and power, but too much force would damage the meat. A crossbow made more sense if the goal was to bring the game back intact.

I removed the bolts loaded into the weapon and replaced them with new ones. I carried around a crossbow because it was handy in various situations. They didn't make any noise, making them superior to firearms for some assassinations.

I took position and fired. True to my aim, the bolt sped through the trees and pierced the Alvanian rabbit's head.

"That's one."

Alvanian rabbits rivaled large dogs in size and made for a substantial meal. I expected everyone to eat a lot, though, so I wanted to get one more.

I finished hunting and trekked back down the mountain. I'd successfully bagged two Alvanian rabbits and one boar. I'd also filled a basket with mushrooms and edible plants.

The Leather Crane Bag is a godsend.

Having to carry all of that without it would have been a pain.

I was going to share the meat with the commoners after I butchered the animals. We weren't going to be able to consume such a large amount by ourselves.

Autumn was fast approaching now, and it was getting time to start thinking about winter. Undoubtedly, this game would help the citizens of the domain.

After I finished cutting up the rabbits and the boar, I handed the pelts of the former and some meat from the latter to an influential man in the village and requested that he share with everyone.

Boar was filling, and if cured in salt, it could help with getting through the winter. Alvanian rabbit pelts went for a high price, so the man was happy to have them.

He gave me fresh vegetables as a thank-you gift. I decided I would use them for the feast tomorrow.

I headed to the kitchen upon returning home. We were holding the feast tomorrow, but preparation needed to be done now.

I needed to rub the meats with spices to disguise their strong scent and let them sit overnight to sink in. It would make the food taste even better.

There were a few people in the kitchen already.

"I'm back. I'm not surprised to see you hard at work with my mom, Tarte, but I didn't expect Dia to join you," I remarked.

"Hey, that hurts. I've been thinking about learning how to cook, too," Dia responded, puffing up her cheeks.

I always took Dia as more of a gourmand than a chef. Her lending a hand with food was rare. I wasn't sure exactly how she was actually assisting, however.

"Ah, welcome back. You've done as splendid a job as ever, Lugh. I don't know how you always find so much delicious meat in such a short amount of time," said Mom.

"The Alvanian rabbit and the boar both look delicious," Tarte commented.

"Did you say Alvanian rabbit?! Please make stew and gratin! That's been my favorite ever since you served it to me all those years ago!" Dia's mouth was practically watering already.

"That's what I'm planning on doing with the rabbit. I'm going to make *tataki* with the boar," I answered.

I'd searched for Alvanian rabbit in the first place to make Dia her favorite cream stew and gratin, so that was already my intention. I intended to prepare *tataki* with the boar because I wanted to test out another new spell as I cooked.

"Lugh, what is *tataki*? I've never heard of it," said Mom.

"That'll be a surprise for tomorrow. Are you all working on fermented runamass?" I questioned.

"That's right. I know how much you and Cian love it," my mother answered.

She and Tarte were preparing fish. Tuatha Dé had a large lake, and as such, its citizens ate a lot of fish-based meals. Runamass, a type of trout, was a signature taste of our domain.

There had long been restrictions on fishing in Tuatha Dé to protect the blessings of nature, and it was banned outright during the breeding season. Thus, the people developed a method of preserving fish to eat during that period.

Initially, the intention was only preservation, but once the Tuatha Dé domain became wealthy around the time of my grandfather's generation, some began to think of using this method to create delicious foods.

Dried runamass dishes made in Tuatha Dé took an extremely long time to prepare using reasonable methods and had quite a distinct taste. They were so good that I was confident they would sell even in the commercial city of Milteu.

Mom and Tarte were making fermented runamass. It was a regional dish in Tuatha Dé produced by fermenting the fish in rice bran made from wheat. This preserved the meat and also intensified the taste. Fermented runamass was excellent steamed, and it was custom to eat it that way on special occasions.

One might find the idea of fermenting fish in rice bran odd, but in my previous world, it wasn't all that rare for people to do so. In principle, it didn't differ much from salted rice malt.

"Wow, this is really nice runamass. It's large and weighty," I observed.

This was an exceptional specimen. You didn't see one this good very often.

"Hans gave it to us as a celebratory gift. With runamass like this, you just have to salt it overnight and steam it!" replied my mother.

"I'm sure it'll be amazing. Although...people from other domains tend not to like it when cooked that way. Shouldn't we fry it since Nevan and Dia are here?" I asked.

In my opinion, salting and steaming only made the runamass more delectable. Unfortunately, fermented dishes were always accompanied by a peculiar scent that many couldn't abide. There were even some in the Tuatha Dé domain who couldn't handle it. Masking that odor was impossible, unfortunately.

Dia and Nevan had never even heard of rice bran, so I estimated an 80 to 90 percent chance they would react negatively. Considering that, it seemed best to fry the runamass with plenty of spices. Admittedly, that did feel like a waste, though.

"Hmm-hmm-hmm, that won't do. I am set on steaming it. You cannot become a Tuatha Dé woman if you don't familiarize yourself with this taste! I'm making you and your father's favorite dish, and you can't convince me otherwise!" she proclaimed, jabbing a finger at the fermenting runamass with great vigor.

She had a point, but I thought it would be best to ease Dia and Nevan into this dish.

That gave me an idea.

"Mom, can you leave the steamed fish to me?"

"...You're definitely plotting something."

"Not at all. I just learned a delicious way of steaming seafood while in Milteu, and I want you to try it. It makes the fish moist without losing any of the flavor. It was so good it made me question all the steamed meals I'd ever eaten in my life. I think fermented runamass would be amazing prepared that way."

"Urgh, I can't help but be interested by that. Fine. But promise me this—you *will* make steamed fish."

"Yeah, no problem," I agreed with a grin.

Saying that I learned this method in Milteu was a lie. It was actually a skill I'd picked up in my previous life. It was the best method for steaming food that I knew. I was sure it would make my mother happy and enable Dia and Nevan to enjoy the runamass as well.

I'd originally learned how to cook to disguise myself as a chef and get near my assassination targets. It was a strange feeling knowing that ability would now bring joy to my mom, girlfriend, and friends.

In my first life, I lived as a tool. But I could say with pride that it hadn't been a waste. The great variety of techniques I gained back then enabled me to put smiles on the faces of my loved ones.

GULP...

Chapter 2 | The Assassin Makes a Delicious Meal

I was in the kitchen the following evening, preparing a feast to celebrate the growth of our family.

"Lord Lugh, please taste the stew."

"Add a little more salt."

"Yes, my lord."

I left the finishing touches on the stew and the salad to Tarte, freeing myself to work on the boar and the runamass.

I pickled the boar in fruit juice containing spices to counteract the smell and enzymes to tenderize the meat. Since noon, I'd been engrossed in a special sort of cooking.

I was using the tenderloin of the boar because it was low in fat, and I had thoroughly removed the muscle.

Given that I was feeding a pregnant woman, I paid particular attention to sanitation. I cleansed the meat thoroughly, performed high-pressure sterilization using wind magic, and froze it to kill parasites using fire magic. Fire magic manipulated quantities of heat, which meant it could also be used to freeze.

I had announced yesterday that I was making *tataki*, but I wasn't going to serve them raw meat.

I was trying out a new cooking utensil. Tarte peered over with great interest.

"That's a strange pot."

"This is called a slow cooker. It's really convenient."

The tool had been a cutting-edge cooking implement in my previous life. It was scientifically proved that sixty degrees Celsius was the ideal temperature to cook meat to increase its flavor and prevent it from becoming tough.

The only problem was that it demanded an incredible amount of time and patience. I needed to heat the boar meat for five hours.

You also have to watch the pot for the entire five hours… But I have a trick to get around that.

The slow cooker had a certain something built into it, which I'd created using technology gleaned from analyzing my divine treasure. I'd engraved a formula into the pot and inserted Fahr Stones into it so the spell would cast repeatedly.

This cooking session was a test of endurance for magic tools to see if they could repeatedly invoke magic over a lengthy period.

I pulled the vacuum-packed boar meat out of the water in the slow cooker. I had poured liquid seasoning and spices into the vacuum seal along with the meat. Five hours in that bag had caused the flavors to permeate the boar.

"Looks perfect. I've learned that extended use over a long period has no negative effect on the precision of a magic tool. Time to finish up."

I grabbed a small charcoal grill I'd once made for fun. The coals were lit, and the grate was heated.

I placed the boar onto the grill. I'd cut the meat into the shape of a cylinder earlier, which allowed me to roll it to sear the entire surface. The meat had already been sufficiently cooked, but I did this for the extra aroma.

Once I finished with that, I cut the boar into thick slices. It had that characteristic tenderness you only got by cooking meat at a lower temperature, plus it had been pickled in fruit enzymes overnight. It would be easy to chew, even in thick slices.

"Wow, what a nice light-pink color. It looks delicious," said Tarte.

"It's great. Here, have a slice," I offered.

Excluding the grilled skin, the boar meat slices were entirely the rose color of the juiciest and most tender roast beef. That was what you could achieve with a slow cooker.

"I can't believe how soft and delicate it is. Boar *tataki* is amazing."

"Yup. The amount of time required prohibits me from making it often, but the taste is worth the effort. Can you finish things up here for me?"

"Yes, my lord!"

Tarte placed the cut slices on a salad and applied a special ponzu sauce as the finishing touch. Ponzu was light and went well with *tataki*.

It was finally time to get started on the day's main course.

"Yep, newcomers are not gonna take well to this scent."

I pulled the runamass out of the rice bran. Unsurprisingly, it stank in that fermented way. You got used to the smell eventually, but it would be rough on anyone eating it for the first time.

I washed the runamass thoroughly to remove the rice bran, cut it open to plaster it with salt, wrapped it in parchment paper that I had moistened together with herbs, and put it in the steam cooker.

Tarte watched me with evident confusion. "Why did you wrap it in paper before steaming?"

"Wrapping the fish in paper keeps it moist and prevents the fish extract from escaping, and it's a good way to transmit an herbal aroma used to remove the smell. It also causes the fish to cook evenly. There are a great number of advantages to this method," I explained.

"That sounds like it will get rid of the smell of the rice bran."

"There's still more to do on that front."

Steaming fish wrapped in paper was a Japanese cooking technique called *hosho-yaki*. This was only the beginning, however. I was making this steamed fish in the Chinese style.

I purposefully removed the runamass from the cooker before it was finished, then moved it onto a different plate. I sprinkled plenty of green onion shreds on top and poured a heated balm on top of that.

A fragrant odor wafted from the loudly crackling charred green onions. That scent mixed with the balm I'd created and the smell of the fermented runamass, removing the rice bran stink entirely.

I'd made the steamed fish a little sweet because I planned to cook it with oil as the last step.

This was a Chinese method known as *qīng zhēng*, and it was one of the most delicious ways to prepare fish.

Lastly, I added sauce and sprinkled coriander on top.

"The charred onion smell is making my mouth water!" exclaimed Tarte.

"The taste is just as good as the smell. The oil made the skin crispy and the exterior soft and flaky, but the middle is moist," I stated.

"Wow, I can't wait to try it. Can I taste it now?"

"No. I want to preserve the visual of the full steaming fish."

"Aw, man."

The fish gave off an appetizing scent and featured the best points of both steamed and fried food. Such was the appeal of *qīng zhēng*.

With that, my feast was now complete.

I'd promised Dia that I would make gratin, but that would definitely make for too much food. I decided I would use the leftovers from the stew to make gratin the next day.

It was finally time to eat. Mom, Dad, Tarte, Dia, and Nevan were all at the table.

Still standing, Tarte inquired, "Um, is it really okay for me to sit at the table?"

"This is a special occasion. We're celebrating! You're already an official mistress, so no one will complain if you receive special treatment. Actually, I would like for you to sit with us from now on," my mother replied.

Tarte sat down and shrank in her chair. She was used to standing behind me as my retainer.

"Um, when did I get officially recognized?" she asked timidly.

My mother chuckled. "Oh, Tarte, I know what you've been up to. I'm floored you thought you could keep such bold behavior from me."

Tarte flushed. She was easy to tease for someone so shy.

"Mom, please save the teasing for later. The food is going to get cold," I said.

"You're right. Let's dig in!"

We all raised a toast with local Tuatha Dé alcohol.

"""""Congratulations on the pregnancy!"""""

After we shared our words of adulation, we began eating.

"Lugh, you lied! There's no gratin!" Dia fumed.

"I thought it would be one too many dishes. I'll make gratin tomorrow," I assured her.

As I'd expected, Dia was puffing out her cheeks in anger. When she tried the boar *tataki*, however, her mood instantly improved.

"This is amazing! I don't think I've ever had meat so soft and sweet."

After watching Dia's reaction, Nevan also reached for a slice of *tataki*.

"I'll have some, too. Oh my, that *is* delicious. This is even more tender than the beef in the capital. Is this really wild boar?" she questioned.

The beef in the capital she was referring to was a luxury food made from cows that were raised specifically for consumption. Most beef came from cows that could no longer work, resulting in tough and smelly meat. Those in the capital, however, lived easy lives so that they wouldn't build extra muscle, and they were only given food that would make them taste better.

"It all depends on the cooking technique. Even wild boar can be delicious if you put enough time and effort into it," I explained.

If you chose an appropriate part of the boar and spent a great deal of effort preparing it, you could make it even better than beef… It wouldn't stand a chance if you spent an equal amount of effort on quality beef, though.

I wanted to find a way to get my hands on a cow from the capital. Maha would probably be able to arrange it for me, but I didn't want to increase her workload for an unnecessary indulgence.

"Is it out of line for me to ask what that 'time and effort' entails, exactly?" Nevan inquired.

"I don't mind sharing a cooking method, and you don't have to keep silent about it, either. I'll write the recipe down for you later," I told her.

I couldn't let her see my slow cooker because it made use of a technique I'd learned from analyzing a divine treasure, and I didn't want that information to spread, but telling her about the method of low-temperature preparation didn't seem problematic. Given the wealth of House Romalung, they could probably hire chefs to work on low-temperature cooking full-time.

"I'm sad there's no gratin, but your stew is as good as ever," Dia praised.

"Lugh's soup is already a specialty of the Tuatha Dé domain, and people even travel from other parts of the country to eat it," Mom said with evident pride.

The wild boar *tataki* and the cream stew were both well-received.

The next dish, the steamed fermented runamass, was what I was nervous about.

My mother narrowed her eyes. "Hmm-hmm-hmm, I see you've yet to touch the fish, Nevan. Any girl unfamiliar with this taste is unfit to marry a Tuatha Dé."

I didn't like the smile on her face. Mom had been wary of Nevan ever since the girl declared yesterday that she would have me marry into her family.

"I would be glad to have some," Nevan responded.

"Wait, that applies to me, too! I can't fathom why anyone would ferment fish in rice bran," said Dia, panicking. She looked way more frightened than Nevan, despite already possessing Mom's approval.

"You said it would stink, but this actually smells quite pleasant. The aroma is only making me more excited to try it," Nevan commented.

Dia gave a surprised look. "This is the fish that was supposed to stink? I thought for sure that hadn't been put on the table yet."

"Huh? Now that you mention it, something *does* smell really nice… Lugh, did you make normal runamass instead of fermenting it? How could you!" accused my mother.

"I promise it's fermented runamass. Try it, and that much will become clear," I assured her.

Fermented fish was known for its awful odor but had a richer taste than raw fish, so she would understand once she tried some. No amount of cooking magic could make a raw dish taste like this.

Nevan, Dia, and my mother grabbed slices and sampled my handiwork.

"It's delectable! This is without a doubt the best steamed fish in the world," declared Nevan.

"Yeah, it's amazing. I've never had fish that smelled this good. It's delicious, too," agreed Dia.

My mother was nodding. "This is unmistakably fermented runamass. It's delicious. This completely spoils my test, but I'm touched that you made such a wonderful meal for me, Lugh. I can feel that the baby in my belly is happy as well."

After hearing their opinions, I decided to taste it myself. Just as I'd wanted, the skin was crispy, the exterior was soft, and the inside was moist. The flavoring was perfect, too. I doubted one could find steamed fish this good even in the capital.

Tarte also gave it high praise after eating some a moment later.

However, one person at the table was looking unsatisfied.

"Do you not like it, Dad?"

"It is certainly good, but...I like the smell of rice bran, so it doesn't feel quite right to me."

That was unexpected. Cooking was a complicated art. I thought the smell of rice bran was a detriment, but apparently, there were some people who liked it.

I was hoping to impress my dad just as much as I was my mom... I'd have to learn from this failure and get it right next time.

For dessert, I served a fruit tart. I'd used an abundance of produce that was in season.

"Whew, that was delicious. You're the best cook in the world, Lugh!" exclaimed my mother.

"Surely that's an exaggeration. You're overly biased as his mother, Esri," my father argued.

"I disagree, Father. As someone who has eaten gourmet food

from all over the world, I assure you he is the best there is. There is more to Sir Lugh than just strength. My lust for him grows ever stronger," said Nevan.

A chill ran down my spine.

My father gave me a strained smile and a look of encouragement. "You're too skilled, Lugh. That is my single greatest worry… The more capable you are, the less likely the country is to ever leave you alone. You should at least take some time to rest while you're at the estate," he urged.

"That's not an option. I need to use this free time to prepare. As I am now, it's only a matter of time before I fail and die."

That was why I had turned today's cooking into a test of endurance for magic tools and the hunting session into a trial for my new probing spell.

"Um, Lord Lugh. We have already killed three demons. I think the last five will be easy for us," Tarte stated.

"You're wrong about that. It will only get tougher from here," I asserted.

That wasn't fear talking—I firmly believed that.

"Oh dear. Do you mind sharing why you believe that?" Nevan pressed. I had a feeling she already had an answer in mind and was checking to see if my thinking matched hers.

"Demons are intelligent. They've been acting individually so far only because they are competing with one another. That rivalry has also made them act hastily in their assaults. But now, three demons—the orc, the beetle, and the lion—have died in succession. Assuming they're not complete morons, the demons have to be devising a plan to deal with us," I explained.

If this was just a game and the demons were the pieces, they would likely continue attacking without much consideration. They weren't that stupid, however. Their methods hadn't worked, so they were bound to change their strategy.

"What do you think they'll do, Lugh?" asked Dia.

"Having two demons attack us at once would be the simplest solution. Do you think we could have won the last battle if there had been a pair of them?" I asked.

Dia frowned. "...I'm afraid we wouldn't have stood a chance."

"That's right. Right now, we can defeat a demon acting alone if we have time for thorough preparation, and even then, it's still a close call. Honestly, I've been worried for a while about the possibility of multiple demons attacking. That's why I devised the version of Gungnir that sends enemies flying."

That was an ability I had initially prepared to separate multiple enemies.

"They are already capable of creating situations I can't handle. Sending a horde of monsters to attack Tuatha Dé, for example. If a demon tried that, I wouldn't be able to abandon my home to track it down. By the time we finished cleaning up the monsters, the demon would have already completed its goal and made its escape. Simpler yet, they could attack a location too far away for us to reach in time."

I could travel at very high speeds with my hang glider. However, we would need to be informed of a demon's appearance first, and the messenger would not move as swiftly as we could. Mina had previously given me information on demons, but there was no guarantee she'd do so again.

"Sounds like a lot could go wrong," said Dia.

"That's why I can't get careless. I need to stay focused," I replied.

I was always striving to become stronger and improve my information network. Presently, I was building a high-speed communication system that shared a base with the Natural You information network I'd constructed with Maha's help.

Until now, I'd been relying on carrier pigeons, which were

considered to be the fastest method in this world. I was now capable of something that far surpassed birds in both speed and reliability.

Real-time transmission would be enormously powerful in this world, where the primary form of long-distance conversation was letter transport. That didn't just go for opposing demons; it would serve me well in my future business endeavors, too.

"You never cease to impress, my lord!" Tarte complimented.

"I appreciate the sentiment, but I want you to grow stronger, too, Tarte," I said.

"I will go through any training for you, no matter how hard!" she responded excitedly.

"I'm gonna work hard as well. I'll keep at my magic development," added Dia.

"Well then, I will contribute with my funds and influence," Nevan remarked.

I smiled. They would make many things possible that I couldn't do alone.

Now that I thought about it, it was nearly time for something I had been anticipating. I needed to prepare.

Chapter 3 The Assassin's Secret Experiment

I had a relaxing and restful morning.

After taking a shower, I retrieved a basket from the kitchen. I was going out this morning, so I prepared lunch for myself in advance.

When I went outside, I found everyone waiting in comfortable clothes.

"I can't wait for the picnic," said Tarte.

Dia nodded in agreement. "And we'll be flying."

"I'm interested to see the other thing you said you had planned," Nevan stated.

There were two goals today.

The first was to fulfill the promise I had made when we returned to Tuatha Dé, which was to teach Dia and Nevan how to pilot a hang glider. There was a small hill on the mountain behind the estate that they would be able to glide comfortably from.

My second goal was to perform a certain experiment. This wasn't a small-scale test like trying out a remodeled spell or testing the endurance of magic tools—it was a test of something that might change the world forever.

"We don't have much time, so let's go. There's a good wind blowing," I urged.

The direction and strength of the wind today were perfect for flying. I was sure they would be able to glide without issue.

I produced two hang gliders with magic and explained how to pilot them.

"All right, get flying."

"Huh?! Do you really expect us to use them right after that explanation?!" Dia asked incredulously.

"He wants us to learn by practice rather than study. It sounds simple enough to me," said Nevan.

"I'll give you directions from the ground, so don't worry," I stated.

It would be rough, but this was the fastest way for the pair to figure it out.

I was only able to use this method because Dia and Nevan were my students. A normal person likely would have crashed and seriously injured themselves or even died. But Dia and Nevan could strengthen themselves with mana if they encountered any difficulty, and even if they did get hurt, I would be able to heal them.

That was why I could get away with being so hard on them.

"Make sure you put on your radio communication devices."

"S-sure thing. They're our safety net, I suppose," responded Dia.

"...I really do wish I could take this technology home and spread it throughout the world," lamented Nevan with a sigh.

They both put on the earpieces. Wearing those would allow me to advise them from the ground.

"Oh yeah, I remember you said these are only effective within one hundred meters," recalled Nevan.

"That only applies if you want to maintain portability and two-way communication. I'm making this mountain the site of my experiment for a prototype I'm testing out."

I produced an object from the ground. It was a large steel magic tool shaped like a rectangle as tall as I was.

"At this size, the device is able to amplify the audio signal. It can reach over two kilometers, twenty times farther than the portable version," I explained.

Because all it could do was bolster the frequency it transmitted, once Dia and Nevan flew beyond one hundred meters, it would no longer be able to receive transmissions from their devices. We would have two-way communication within one hundred meters, but it would be one-sided beyond that.

Being able to advise them was still handy, though.

"It can reach that far?! This would make anyone unbeatable in war. It would enable instantaneous transmission of information to an entire army at once. This is more valuable than ten thousand soldiers!" Nevan said, amazed.

Even an army of that size would be able to act with perfect unity with this. Such a development would bolster the fighting strength of any force by a dozen times over, perhaps even more.

"As I've told you, I didn't make these for war. If the nobles of this country obtained this technology, it would take them two seconds before they put it to use invading other nations," I said.

There were many aristocrats of great ambition in the Alvanian Kingdom. It was inevitable that such hot-blooded people would launch campaigns against other territories were they to acquire something so powerful.

Nevan pulled a face. "What is the problem with that? It would lead to greater prosperity for this kingdom."

"That's not my style. I would rather bring prosperity to the country by improving what we have than by stealing from others."

I wasn't a pacifist, but I didn't want to cause unnecessary misery and bloodshed. I was personally content with the Tuatha Dé domain alone, and I was not going to get roped into mass killing just to satisfy another's greed.

"Your lack of ambition may be your one weakness, Sir Lugh," Nevan commented.

"I don't see that as a failing. Anyway, forget that. Get flying before the wind stops blowing," I instructed.

"S-sure. Help me if I need it, okay?" Dia requested.

Looking much more confident, Nevan said, "Here I go."

The pair took off from the top of the hill. They rode the wind and glided far into the distance. They were both flying safely and with solid fundamentals.

"Dia and Nevan are fast learners. I knew it would be okay not to go with them," I remarked.

"They really are. They got the hang of it much quicker than I did," agreed Tarte.

They were even swift to correct whenever a crosswind hit. Their understanding of the structure of the hang gliders was what allowed them to fly so well.

However, they both steadily dropped in altitude because they couldn't use wind magic. There weren't many updrafts to regain height.

Eventually, both Dia and Nevan landed. They strengthened their bodies with mana and began to run back this way.

Actually, Dia clearly had something else in mind. I didn't like the face she was making.

I have a bad feeling about this.

"What's she doing now...?"

My girlfriend ran full speed and then jumped as high as she could. From that elevation, she was sure to fall right back down.

She started an incantation midair.

Under typical circumstances, intoning magic took all of your mana and resources and made it so that you would be unable to maintain physical strengthening, but the use of Quick Chant, which was derived from Multi-Chant, enabled her to do both at once.

Dia could not use wind magic, so I had no idea what she was plotting.

"Whoa!"

A massive explosion erupted behind Dia. She rode the blast to lift the hang glider's elevation and accelerate.

She set off the detonation a good distance behind her so that it wouldn't damage the hang glider. What's more, she was using Multi-Chant to begin another spell concurrently with the explosive magic.

The second bit of magic activated.

"...She's absolutely crazy."

Flames were shooting out of the soles of her feet.

Technically, it wasn't fire. Dia gathered air, pressurized it, and combusted it to spew hot and pressurized gas for thrust. Her method operated similarly to the workings of a jet engine.

She managed greater speed than even Tarte and I could, and we could manipulate the wind.

I was astonished that Dia had come up with such a spell despite never hearing of a jet engine.

"Lady Dia is amazing. She's going so fast," Tarte said in wonder.

"Don't get any ideas about imitating her. That has a high degree of difficulty and must be very unruly. Losing control even a little bit would cause the flames to burn up the hang glider, and then you'd be in free fall. The mana consumption must be terrible, too. Anyone other than Dia or me would run out of power immediately."

Because Dia couldn't use wind magic, she had to employ a non-elemental spell to gather the wind around her and compress it. This was an extremely inefficient method.

There were many flaws, but putting those aside, it was a very good spell. If I replicated it, my ability to alter air with magic would eliminate the need to gather and compress it.

After spending some time enjoying flying, Dia descended and landed next to us.

"Ha-ha-haaaa. What'd you think of that? I can fly fast even without wind magic!"

"You surprised me. I may have to make a special hang glider for you."

"Thanks, I'd appreciate it."

"Don't even think about trying to fly to the capital alone."

"Th-that would be pretty difficult."

It was terribly inefficient magic. It wouldn't last long enough.

Nevan returned shortly afterward, carrying her hang glider.

"Haah...haah... I'm finally back. Flying feels terrific, but the return trip is torture. It's so heavy," she said, panting. The ever-elegant Nevan was drenched in sweat. "Dia, I have a request," she began.

"What is it?" Dia responded.

"Can you create a propulsion spell with light magic?"

"Sorry, I can't imagine how I would do that."

Light propulsion was often seen in science fiction, but I had never heard of it being realized. Technically, a specialized agency had announced a completed theory that proved it was possible. I didn't feel like even I would have a chance of recreating it with magic, though.

"That's unfortunate..."

Magic was helpful, but it wasn't almighty. There were things that it wasn't capable of.

◇

After enjoying our fill of gliding, we sat down to eat lunch. It wasn't quite time for what I was waiting for.

"I'm thrilled that we are getting to taste your cooking again, Sir Lugh," said Nevan.

"I wish you would cook every day," added Dia.

Tarte looked down. "Um, that would make me kind of sad. I would feel inadequate as his retainer."

I unveiled the sandwiches in the basket. I'd prepared standard egg sandwiches, pork steak burgers with wild boar meat, and a special surprise for today.

"Lugh, you lied again. Yesterday, you said you would make gratin. Urgh, I want to eat gratin so badly...," Dia moaned, looking at me with obvious ire.

"Well, I don't think gratin would work on a picnic... It wouldn't be very good after it got cold," Tarte asserted.

"What is gratin?" asked Nevan.

Dia proudly took charge of answering.

"It's delicious. First, you simmer macaroni in the cream stew we ate yesterday, then you add cheese and bake it in the oven. It has a very rich and satisfying taste. It's my favorite food."

"That does sound tasty."

"And yet, a certain someone refuses to make it."

Dia shot me a look again.

"Have a little faith in me, Dia. I did make some. Try the sandwiches first."

I hadn't lied. I was Dia's boyfriend, and I wanted to make her happy. That said, gratin was still ill-suited to an outdoor meal.

That was why I made gratin that would taste good even after it got cold.

"All I see are sandwiches," Dia protested.

"Let's start eating!" exclaimed Tarte.

"Yes, let's," agreed Nevan.

I smiled and poured soup out of a flask.

Nevan took a bite. "Wow, this egg sandwich has a rich taste. It's a little sour. I've never tasted anything like it."

All I did was crush soft-boiled eggs and mix them with homemade mayonnaise, but mayonnaise didn't exist in this world. That made for a novel flavor that would garner positive reception anywhere.

"The seasoning on the pork steak is salty and sweet. It's fantastic," observed Tarte.

I'd cooked the steak in the teriyaki style, which meant marinating it in soy sauce and broiling it. Teriyaki was good even when it was cold.

Last but not least, it was finally time for today's surprise item.

"Hey, it's gratin! You really made gratin! It's soooo good." Dia squealed like a child.

The special surprise was gratin croquette sandwiches. I'd added meat and macaroni to cream stew, then used that as the main ingredient to make deep-fried croquettes. The croquettes were covered with thick tomato sauce that I'd boiled as long as possible and then placed between pieces of bread.

The result was a strong flavor that could be enjoyed even when the sandwich had cooled.

"Gratin is very delicious indeed," praised Nevan.

Dia puffed up her chest. "It's not my favorite food for nothing."

"I like it, too," Tarte concurred.

Carb-heavy pasta and carb-heavy white sauce coated in carb-heavy batter and deep-fried, and then sandwiched in carb-heavy bread. I felt like you might find a picture of this meal in the dictionary next to *carbohydrate*.

Despite all that, it was truly delicious. It didn't make sense. In my previous world, you could even find gratin croquette burgers at a particular massively popular hamburger restaurant.

"Whew, that was delicious. You really are the best boyfriend in the world, Lugh."

"I'm glad you liked it."

I stroked Dia after she hugged me. Seeing her this happy made the effort I'd put into the meal worthwhile.

"Oh yeah, you said you were conducting another important experiment not related to hang gliding, right?" she questioned.

"Yeah, it's about time I get to it, too," I responded after checking my pocket watch to confirm that it was nearing the appointed time.

An experiment that could change this world forever was about to begin. This technology would allow me to be notified the moment a demon was found.

The giant rectangular communication device I had used to talk with Dia and Nevan began to vibrate.

"Can you hear me, dear brother? This is your little sister calling from Milteu with love."

Maha's voice arrived in real time from about four hundred kilometers away.

"I can hear you. The experiment was a success."

"Hee-hee, I'm so glad. Now I'll be able to hear your voice anytime."

The experiment was a success.

I had set out to make a telephone. This project actually began two years ago, and I'd finished the prototype back then as well. However, establishing a proper telecommunications network required time, money, and labor. Even making full use of Natural You's influence and funds, it took this long to complete.

The girls were shocked. Transmitting a signal over a distance of two kilometers was hard enough for them to believe. They could never have imagined four hundred kilometers.

This tool could only send a signal two kilometers earlier in the day, but now we could hear Maha's voice from four hundred kilometers away. It was time to explain to them how I had pulled this off.

Chapter 4 | The Assassin's Telecommunications Network

Maha continued to speak through the large device I'd created.

"I'm so moved. After two years, our work is finally complete. This sounded like nothing more than a fantasy when you first told me about it."

"I'm sure it did. But now all the principal sites are connected, and the telecommunications network is complete," I said.

"This will make Natural You unbeatable. I'll use this to give you more support than ever, dear brother."

Building this had taken a considerable portion of time and effort. We'd faced many obstacles along the way and patiently solved them one by one.

As part of the experiment, Maha gave me a business update and read the results of an investigation I'd requested. There were zero problems with the sound quality.

If I had to look for a slight issue, there was a tiny bit of lag because of the distance of the transmission.

"Am I imagining things, or am I hearing the voice of a girl I don't know behind you? I also get the feeling that she's lovely and harbors special feelings for you… Hee-hee, the idea that you went and got yourself a new girlfriend while I was working myself near to death for you is so funny I might cry."

Maha and I concluded with a personal conversation before ending the call.

That was terrifying. What really scared me was that Maha didn't even sound angry, just completely exhausted. She hung up without even listening to my excuses. I would have to go meet her in person soon. I asked the unreasonable of her every single day. I needed to make sure I looked after her.

Nevan hounded me for answers as soon as my conversation with Maha was over.

"Did that really come from Milteu?! That's just under four hundred kilometers from here. Are you playing a prank on us? There isn't a girl hiding in that box, is there?"

"I would never waste my time doing something so frivolous. Her voice actually traveled here from that distance."

Nevan was speechless. Such range would enable much more than ordering an army on a battlefield; this could be used to connect people throughout the entire country. There was no way she didn't see the possibilities.

Information had degrees of freshness.

Take business as an example. If you knew the market prices throughout a city at all times, you would be able to rake in enormous wealth just by moving goods from one spot to the next. However, because information needed time to travel, people couldn't do that. By the time you procured some items, the market price may have already changed, or you might wind up in competition with others who had the same idea.

However, if you possessed a telecommunications network, you would be able to send and receive information instantaneously. That meant you would be able to deliver goods prior to changes in the market price and before rival companies had a chance to act. Even a monkey would be able to turn a profit.

The advantages spread beyond the business world. In every field, from politics to military affairs and more, instant data would allow you to view the world more comprehensively than those without it.

The ability to move a few days faster than the opposition would always give you a leg up.

The people of this world were not connected. News took longer to reach those who were farther from the source. We were going to be the only ones genuinely in touch with the world, granting us unparalleled coordination.

It was an advantage beyond what anyone in this world could conceive of. This invention would change the world.

"...If used to its full potential, this would enable world domination," said Nevan.

"If that was our goal, yes. But as I explained earlier, I have no desire to do anything like that. I developed this only as a tool to strengthen my information network," I responded.

Outside of employing it for Natural You, I had no intention to use it as anything other than a relay device.

"Um, Lord Lugh. How are you able to communicate over that far a distance? Two kilometers was the limit for that big box... Do you have something even bigger somewhere around here?!" asked Tarte incredulously.

"Ah, I'm curious about that, too," Dia admitted.

Tarte and Dia recovered from the shock much more quickly than Nevan. They didn't understand the value of this invention as she did.

Tarte's question must have been on all of their minds.

"I was using a wireless version before, but this one is wired. The signal travels through cables that connect the devices. That's why they can transmit so much farther than the wireless version," I explained.

Dia looked around. "I don't see a cable anywhere."

"That's because it's underground," I answered.

That was the biggest reason this had taken two long years to complete.

"Aren't you worried about the wires, my lord? If one got cut somewhere, the devices wouldn't work," Tarte pointed out.

"You're right about that. That's why I made cables that wouldn't break. This is what they are made out of."

"It's thicker than my legs," Tarte observed, astounded.

"The part that's actually transmitting the signal is thin, but it's protected by ample material. I'll show you how sturdy this is. Try as hard as you can to cut it. You can even strengthen yourself with mana."

"O-okay, I'll give it a shot!"

I held out the wire with both hands, and Tarte drew her knife and slashed it. Her boosted strength made the impact powerful. Her knife was a magic blade crafted from a special alloy I'd fashioned. The blow would have cut through iron, yet the cable rebuked her attack.

Tarte's eyes were wide with clear surprise. "No way. It didn't break."

"That's how strong it is. This wire can handle Tarte's hits. It's also soft enough to bend so that it won't snap. And not only that, the cables are buried at least five meters underground. They're tough to cut, and I've devised a way for the devices to function even if one is severed," I elaborated.

"What do you mean by that?" Dia pressed.

"Two different routes connect the important sites. If one is disrupted, the signal will travel along the other."

I'd designated Milteu and Tuatha Dé as core sites, so they were connected by both an east and a west route.

Dia arched an eyebrow. "Wait, 'important sites' suggests that there are other less critical ones."

"Of course. There are twenty sites in total set up with a communication device. There is already one stationed in each of the kingdom's major cities," I said.

"Does that mean a voice can travel from one of the devices to any of the other nineteen?" asked Dia.

"That's right."

Anything less and it wouldn't have been a network.

The maximum distance the wired devices could transmit a signal was eighty kilometers, meaning no sites could be farther than that from another. Once a transmission reached one device, it could amplify the signal and send it on to the next one, enabling communication over a distance of hundreds of kilometers.

The reason I'd prepared two routes was not just in case a wire was broken, but also in anticipation of a site's destruction.

"The scale of this is unreal. I can see why it took two whole years," said Dia.

"That was part of it, but having to build it in secret made it take much longer than it would have otherwise. I couldn't just hire anybody for this. I needed mages who could wield earth magic, a significant number of them. I used forty percent of Natural You's total assets to build this telecommunications network," I explained.

"U-um, forty percent of Natural You's assets could buy you a small castle, right?" asked Tarte.

"More than that. The price was significantly more than you're imagining, Tarte," I answered.

It wasn't easy finding mages who would agree to such dirty work *and* be tight-lipped about it, and the ones I did locate had charged an exorbitant sum.

I'd made the telephone lines and the equipment myself, but most of the money still went to labor costs and bribing people in power to turn a blind eye.

"Whoa, that's an absurd amount of funds," said Dia.

"It sure was. I'm not concerned, though. Now that the telecommunications network is complete, I can make that back in two months."

That wasn't wishful thinking. It was the minimum amount I expected to make in that time. By my estimations, I would actually pull in even more than that.

That was the kind of profit I could reap by dominating my competition in an information war.

"Two months? You're being overly modest. One week should be enough. I'm surprised you decided to share this with me. House Romalung would be willing to destroy a city or two for something like this. Actually, make that an entire country," stated Nevan.

"I know you won't take it from me by force. You believe that my value is even higher. Don't you want to see even greater marvels?"

"Hee-hee, you're like a chicken that lays golden eggs… Very well, I will keep this strictly to myself. Truly, you never cease to amaze." Nevan smiled. She then began to grumble to herself about how effectively she would use this telecommunications network.

"There's one other thing I'm wondering about. You used a wireless connection to advise us while we were flying earlier. Could this machine take a wired transmission delivered from another site and then send that signal wirelessly to a mobile device?" Dia inquired.

"Very sharp. That's exactly right. The reverse is possible as well. You can only transmit one hundred meters with a mobile device, but that information can be picked up by one of the wired ones and delivered to a different site," I answered.

I was impressed that Dia had deduced that on her own. I'd

created both stationary and mobile communication tools specifically for that purpose.

The large wired apparatuses could transmit to all mobile ones in the surrounding region. That meant you could receive transmissions even if you weren't at one of the hubs, and you could also send information to one of those sites from a distance.

This was the same way cell phones worked in my old world. Communication machines were set up in every city to send data to cell phones, and the machines were connected to other devices by wires.

The convenience of that system was one of the reasons I'd set it up this way, but more importantly, this enabled me to get away with not telling my intelligence agents the exact location of the large stationary devices.

I'd given my agents mobile phones, but I concealed the existence of the base units. I'd also informed them that the phones were excavated divine treasures rather than my own inventions. All they were aware of was that using their phones at specific locations let them transmit information across the country.

It wouldn't especially matter if any of them betrayed me, because I didn't mind if they told anyone the phones were divine treasures, nor did I care if they were stolen.

I only chose people I could trust to be my intelligence agents, but there was nothing wrong with being careful.

"Whoa, that's amazing," Tartc said.

"That's why I want you to keep these communication devices with you at all times. They'll allow you to contact me from most cities. Also, even if I'm not at any of the sites when you contact me, I can listen to a day's worth of transmissions afterward," I explained.

"Yes, my lord. I'll take care of it," Tartc responded.

"Wow, I'll make sure not to lose it," added Dia.

"I will never let go of it," promised Nevan.

The three gripped their mobile communication tools.

Teaching the girls how to use them could wait. There were different channels, and each one served a different purpose. I'd made their mobile phones to only receive transmissions from my private channels.

"All right, the experiment is complete. Let's head back," I declared.

"Ah, I'll go back with my hang glider," stated Dia.

"I will use mine, too. That way, I won't have to carry it," Nevan said.

"Fine with me."

Evidently, they had taken a great liking to the hang gliders. I watched as they flew off.

My personal phone rang. The channel being used was the one for my intelligence agents in the royal capital.

I listened to the report.

Tarte looked frightened as she commented, "Um, you look like something is upsetting you, my lord."

"Sorry, I just got some bad news. It seems my network is coming in handy already. It likely would have been too late had this news reached me in three days. The jealousy of nobles is truly disgraceful."

Receiving information in real time was just as valuable as anticipated. I hadn't been wrong to make this investment.

I planned to use my swift access to this new information to take those idiots in the capital unawares. My strike would come quicker than they could imagine.

Chapter 5 | The Assassin Prepares a Counterstrike

I returned to the estate and got right to work on my retaliation against the aristocrats who had laid a trap for me.

If left to play out, their ploy would harm both my individual standing and House Tuatha Dé.

"Building a telecommunications network with well-placed agents has given me even more power than I expected."

It was an enormous infrastructure that connected twenty major cities and allowed for one-to-one conversation. I had deployed spies to each area, and they used the phones to share the information they gathered. Specifically, there were two types of people I dispatched for the job.

The first group was made up of the most loyal of my Natural You employees. They were working as merchants in all the important metropolises, and they primarily sent me data related to economics and the distribution of goods. Overseeing the flow of money and inventory helped me recognize the start of any schemes.

The greater the plot, the more funds and assets will shift. I can use that to deduce whatever the planner is up to.

Keeping people quiet was easy compared to disguising shifting resources.

It was the other group that proved helpful this time.

My other intelligence agents consisted of nobles who admired me as the Holy Knight. Nearly all of them were mages, and they offered intel pertaining to noble society.

They were made up of people who could contact the Holy Knight, so they were highly skilled. The only people capable of that were either from highly ranked houses or were those with access to unsavory back channels.

I had interviewed each candidate individually and chose the ones I could trust to become my operatives.

Using them was easy. They looked up to the Holy Knight as a hero, and aiding me made them feel like heroes themselves. I also paid them plenty of money. They may have been nobles, but most of them had not yet inherited their houses and thus had never possessed much to spend for themselves, so they were happy to have funds.

I also secured their loyalty using conditioning techniques and reduced the risk of estrangement by giving them whatever their positions required. That would ensure they would give me all the information I could want about their own houses.

The problem was that while they were skilled, many of them were childish. They were all people who wanted to play at being heroes, so that attitude was unavoidable. As a result, I invested a lot of effort into risk management in the event any of them were discovered.

"Prioritizing observation of the royal capital paid off."

I had deployed many agents there. It was the center of politics, and the nobles who valued the central government over their own domains were extraordinarily vain and prone to bouts of jealousy.

I suspected there would be many in the capital plotting my downfall. Certain aristocrats were undoubtedly beside themselves with jealousy over me.

According to the hierarchy, I was no more than the oldest son of a lowly baron's house. Yet I was killing one demon after another, the royal family liked me, and even House Romalung, one of the four major dukedoms, was getting friendly with me. All that glory and favor was bound to attract envious glares.

These nobles were afraid that House Tuatha Dé would climb the ranks of the nobility and threaten their own positions. If only they knew that Dad and I both had no interest in that kind of thing.

"If they thought about this even a little, even they should understand what would happen if they sabotaged my position."

They would only be harming themselves if they got rid of someone capable of defeating demons. The hero was currently unable to leave the capital, meaning the demons would be free to rampage all over Alvan if I was unable to deal with them.

The demons being left to do as they wished would result in the resurrection of the Demon King. It was entirely possible that not even the hero would be able to defeat the Demon King, which would mean the destruction of the kingdom.

Those aristocrats should've at least left me alone until the demon threat was taken care of.

Despite the grave stakes, they justified their savage acts born of jealousy and vanity with unfathomable logic as they plotted my downfall.

"I had planned to let stuff like this go if it wasn't overly harmful."

This particular scheme was of especially poor character. I had to deal with it.

I was going to challenge them openly at first, but I was considering turning to my main profession if required. That was how deplorable their trap was.

The following day, a Romalung messenger arrived to pick up Nevan. As a lady of a prestigious family, she was constantly busy. She had remained with us as long as she could, but it was time to see her off.

"I enjoyed my time here in Tuatha Dé very much. I will come again. Thank you for your hospitality," she said.

"You gave us a great time in Romalung, so there's no need for thanks. I hope we can continue to build a favorable relationship," I responded.

"As do I. Next time we meet, I'll treat you as your caring upperclassman."

"And I'll behave as your innocent junior."

That reminded me that the academy's reconstruction was supposed to finish soon. That would indeed make Nevan my upperclassman again. I'd intentionally avoided her at the academy last time, but there would no longer be any need for that.

"Before I go, I noticed that something seems to be troubling you, Sir Lugh," Nevan remarked.

"What are you talking about?" I responded.

"Don't think you can fool me. Nothing about your expression or your behavior suggests that anything has changed, but something feels different."

She got me. Very few people in this life or my previous one had ever seen through me when I concealed my feelings.

"A little trouble came up."

"Shall I lend you some of House Romalung's strength?"

"I can handle it myself."

That wasn't a boast. I genuinely didn't require Nevan's help, and I didn't want to wind up indebted to her.

I wouldn't need House Romalung's help until later on.

"I see. Please contact me if you change your mind… I will keep this on me at all times," she said, waving her mobile phone.

"When the time comes, I will," I responded.

This telecommunications network was set up in each of the kingdom's major cities. It went without saying that included the Romalung domain.

I had taught Nevan the location of the large signal device in the city, and we would be able to contact each other if she used it. Her phone was set to access only one channel, however, preventing her from listening in on my intelligence agents.

Nevan gave one last bow and departed.

Being around her was mentally exhausting, but it was also great fun, and I learned a lot from her. Maintaining an amicable relationship with Nevan was for the best.

After Nevan left, I returned to my room and used my mobile phone to connect to the telecommunications network.

There was a large relay device set up within the Tuatha Dé estate. It was a slightly special one and not present in the records. Even Maha didn't know about it.

This machine had a unique function that the others didn't have. Its purpose was to pinpoint any traitors and keep the damage they caused to a minimum. That was why I kept everyone in the dark about it.

I set my phone to one of the channels established to speak to my intelligence agents rather than the personal one for the girls.

"This is Silver, speaking to King..."

I used real names when speaking on our personal channels, but I used code names when talking to my operatives. I was Silver, and King referred to my agents in the royal capital.

I issued my orders to begin setting a ploy for the fools trying to trap me.

I prepared hang gliders the next day. The first was a two-person one for Dia and me, and the other was for Tarte alone.

"Sorry about this. I had wanted to rest at home for a little longer," I apologized.

"I don't mind at all! I will go anywhere if it means I can be with you, my lord," Tarte responded.

"This is really terrible. I can't believe they're calling you a criminal," said Dia.

"Yeah, it's despicable."

The people trying to bring me down were framing me for murder. They hadn't discovered that I was an assassin, so their claim was an utter fabrication.

There was no greater shame for one of my profession than being discovered and captured. It was as good as being publicly branded as unskilled.

Even if this was a false charge, it still infuriated me.

"Their methods are crude. They killed a political rival and disposed of the corpse in Jombull, and they are going to have a false witness testify that I slew the person during the battle with the demon," I explained.

"Um, would you really be punished for that, my lord? I think it's inevitable that people will die during a fight with a demon. If we were focused on preventing all loss of life, we wouldn't be able to fight," said Tarte.

"I shouldn't be. As a Holy Knight, I'm relieved of the responsibility for any damage I cause during battle," I answered.

Those rights didn't just apply to a Holy Knight but also to the hero and some of the higher-ranking regular knights.

When people of great strength fought, it was inevitable that there would be far-reaching destruction. People in those positions were often deployed to fight powerful enemies or to deal with extreme emergencies. They wouldn't be able to handle the situations properly if they were worried about collateral damage.

"That doesn't make sense, then. It shouldn't be possible to pin the crime on you," reasoned Dia.

"No, it's enough for them. The person they're saying I killed was virtuous and popular. Even if ending their life isn't technically a crime, I'll become an object of hatred among the commoners and nobles. Some may even call for vengeance. The scheming aristocrats want to sabotage my standing. They're even fabricating discord between the victim's family and House Tuatha Dé to make it look like I killed him on purpose."

Some death may have been accepted as inevitable due to my rights as the Holy Knight, but intentional murder would still be judged problematic. Even if I wasn't charged with a crime, there was no doubt that many noble houses would place a variety of sanctions on House Tuatha Dé.

"That's disgusting. This is why I hate noble society," said Dia.

The most effective way to advance in the aristocracy was to drag down those above you.

It was possible for people to climb in rank during a war by rendering distinguished service, but it was much more difficult to stand out in times of peace. That meant the most important things for aristocrats became avoiding failure and causing their rivals above them to drop in the standings. Particularly ambitious nobles excelled in that area.

The people plotting my downfall were of that variety.

"How do you plan to deal with it, my lord?" asked Tarte.

"I've discovered the identity of the witness who is going to provide false testimony. I'll win him over to our side with a little *convincing*. When it comes time to tell everyone of my crime, he will instead testify against the mastermind who is trying to sabotage me," I explained.

"He's going to change allegiances?" asked Tarte.

"You think I can't manage it?"

Tarte seemed surprised, but I was a master of persuasion.

I wouldn't have had time for this counterstrike without my telecommunications network because of how trials worked in the Alvanian Kingdom.

After someone accused another person of a crime, there was a deliberation to determine if a trial should be held. Upon approval, a carrier pigeon would be sent with a letter, and a government official would depart in a carriage at the same time, carrying a copy of the same letter.

The accused had to return to their domain within three days of the government official's arrival and then accompany the official to the capital. Then the trial was held as soon as possible, taking into account the involved parties' schedules.

It took a minimum of one week to reach Tuatha Dé from the capital by carriage. A carrier pigeon would arrive in two to three days.

Thus, the government official would arrive five days after the bird. The official would then wait for three days, giving the accused a total of eight days after receiving the initial letter to return to their domain and go with them to the capital.

However, this time, it seemed like the plan was for the carrier pigeon to have an "unfortunate accident" that prevented it from delivering the missive. Ignorant of the situation, I wouldn't return to the Tuatha Dé domain during the three days when the official was there. This would make me a truant, and my guilt would be automatically assumed.

Even in the case that I made it, the people taking me to court had pulled some strings to have the trial take place the day after I reached the capital. If I hadn't known about the conspiracy, I would've either lost the case by default or had to attend the trial with no chance for any preparation.

"This really wasn't what I had in mind when I built this telecommunications network," I admitted with a bitter laugh.

Still, it had saved me. The government official carrying the letter had reportedly left the capital this morning. Learning about that yesterday afforded me a bit of preparation time.

"I'm relieved that it sounds like you can prove your innocence," Dia remarked.

"Me too. But I don't plan to end things there. They're going to pay."

It wouldn't be enough to simply prove my innocence. I needed to make an example of those who plotted against me so that no one would be foolish enough to attempt such a thing again.

Chapter 6 | The Assassin Puts On a Disguise

We were flying to the capital on our hang gliders, moving much more swiftly than we would have on the road.

A trip to the royal capital by carriage required days. Quick information and movement were what gave me the edge on my opponents.

At some point, the pleasant flight began to make me feel a bit mischievous.

"I'm gonna try the spell you created, Dia," I stated.

Her spell used a system built on sound logic that ejected pressurized air heated by flames to gain extreme acceleration. That Dia created this with no prior knowledge of jet propulsion showed her incredible sense for magic.

I would be able to make even better use of it, however.

"Be careful. I didn't like the sound the hang glider made when I tried it. You can use wind magic, so I doubt the hang glider would hold if you went all out," Dia warned

"I'm calculating the intensity carefully," I assured her.

I'd made the hang gliders as light as possible so they offered the least resistance when accelerated with wind magic. There was a bit of leeway, but if I went above the top velocity the glider could handle, there would be a risk of damage.

"Did you already finish your version of the spell?" Dia inquired.

I nodded. "Yeah, before we left."

It seemed like it would come in handy, so I'd put together a modified version of Dia's formula.

I'd made two revisions. The first was to use wind magic to gather the air around me more efficiently. The second was to add a non-elemental spell to cover the hang glider in a coating that shielded it from the propulsive force.

I called the revised bit of magic Thruster.

It would come in handy for both travel and battle. The high-pressure gas I expelled would be extremely lethal, and it would enable me to perform powerful attacks while moving at very high speeds.

It was time to test Thruster out.

I used Multi-Chant to twine together fire and wind mana, then finished the incantation for Thruster and activated the spell.

We accelerated with astounding speed, our faces distorting from the wind pressure. We were moving ridiculously fast. It felt so good that I could see myself getting addicted to it.

I ended Thruster just a few seconds later. Any more and I worried the glider might fall apart.

"This spell is incredible," I said.

"Ah-ha-ha, that was amazing! That's what happens when you combine my work with wind magic and your outrageous mana capacity," Dia cheered.

"It seems that way… I'll have to redesign the hang glider so I can make effective use of this."

I would need to increase its sturdiness enough to withstand the incredible velocity, even if it made it heavier. Constructing a frame to handle Thruster made more sense than holding back on the spell's strength.

"That would be nice, but I don't think there would be any

point if you're the only one who can use it. Look, we can't even see Tarte anymore," Dia said.

"You have a point there."

I quit using wind magic and switched to just gliding to give Tarte time to catch up. After a short wait, I heard her voice on the radio.

"I lost sight of you after you *whoosh*ed ahead... I can't keep up with that at all..."

It sounded like she was in tears.

As Dia had claimed, Thruster was pointless if we got separated.

Wait, I'm going about this the wrong way.

"Okay, I know what I'll do. I'll make a four-person aircraft designed with Thruster in mind."

I'd initially built gliders instead of an airplane because I couldn't manage the necessary propulsion and because I could move faster by prioritizing lightness. According to my mental calculations, however, Thruster would allow superior speed even if I increased the aircraft's weight and designed it for four passengers.

"...What kind of monstrous thing are you going to make? You're scaring me a little," Dia commented.

"You'll have to wait and see," I answered.

The final product would no longer be a hang glider, but a private jet.

I would need to work out a design.

We landed on the outskirts of the royal capital. I wasn't the only one in disguise this time; Dia and Tarte were as well. I did their makeup and chose their clothes.

I'd also prepared fake identification papers. We could have

gotten into the city using our academy IDs, but our goal with this trip was to win over the witness of my would-be saboteurs. I couldn't risk anyone realizing that we had visited the royal capital.

Frowning, Dia said, "I don't like dyeing my hair. I hope you haven't damaged it."

"Don't worry. I took that into account. This is a new Natural You product," I assured her.

I was very fond of Dia's silver locks. I would never do anything to harm them.

I had developed this dye as merchandise for my cosmetics brand. There was a demand for hair coloring among the wealthy, both for hiding grays and for achieving more fantastic beauty.

The selling point for all of Natural You's products was that they were as good for your health as they were for your looks. That was why it reigned as the top company on the market.

I had designed this dye so that it would actually provide care for your hair instead of harm it, and it flew off the shelves after word about it spread.

"That disguise is unbelievable. Everything about you feels different, Lady Dia," observed Tarte.

Tarte herself had long, straight red hair. I'd used a binder to flatten her chest and gave her the makeup of a pampered lady. She appeared nothing like her usual self. Her easy-to-approach atmosphere was gone, replaced by that of a young woman of noble birth.

After looking at Tarte, Dia checked a mirror.

"...I don't care too much for the neck up, but would it be bad if I wore the rest of the disguise every day from now on?" she asked.

"Yes. That would bring you no satisfaction," I answered.

Dia's hair was black, and she was wearing it up. I used her cosmetics to intentionally dirty her fair skin and give her freckles to give her the appearance of a country girl. By contrast, I dressed her in expensive and gaudy clothes.

Anyone who saw her would think the girl was just some rural person enjoying a trip to the capital.

There wasn't a trace of her usual noble, doll-like beauty. The facade completely spoiled her good looks. That she was still cute was a testament to her natural fairness.

Dia, however, wasn't focused at all on her face. She couldn't take her eyes off her chest, which I had padded to look bigger.

"I can't believe how real this looks. You should offer this at Natural You. It would definitely sell! I would totally buy this!"

"...Yeah, it probably would."

Some upper-class women stuffed their busts, but it was always crude and easy to spot. They could fool people to an extent if they wore thick dresses, but the padding felt too different from the real thing. It was unnatural.

However, the lining I'd fashioned, combined with a special bra, made the fake chest look entirely real. The shape and texture were perfect. Even touch wasn't enough to figure out it was fake. Initially, I'd created the false bust for assassination, without considering the potential sales.

"This is the best. They're soft, and they even bounce. I love them so much. I can finally say things I've *always* wanted to say! 'Having a large chest is really hard on my shoulders.' 'Running makes them bounce, which is painful and makes me lose my balance.' 'These are just a hindrance.'"

Dia looked very satisfied with herself as she complained about her new chest. Despite her gripes, she seemed to be taking great delight in this.

For some reason, Tarte's face was flushed. I then realized that Dia was mimicking Tarte's voice.

"Lady Dia, that's mean! Those are all things that I've said!"

"Heh-heh, this is payback. Now you understand the anger and pain the less-endowed feel when they hear those words!"

Dia was a near-perfect human being with one insecurity: the size of her chest. I decided I should let her have her moment.

I worked on my disguise as I watched the two girls banter.

"All right, let's get going. Be careful not to lose your fake identification. We can't enter the capital without it," I announced.

Tarte blinked a few times. "...Um, is that really you, my lord? You couldn't look more like a girl. You're more beautiful than me... I think I'm in shock."

"Me too. I've never seen a girl this beautiful, even at parties here in the capital," agreed Dia.

I was cross-dressing. Being a woman better suited my plan.

My physical appearance was relatively androgynous, and with a good enough disguise, I could pull off a perfect feminine figure. I was sure of my acting as well.

When I was a young boy in my previous life, I would sometimes dress as a girl to seduce and kill my targets.

"You made this fake chest originally so you could look like a girl, didn't you?" asked Dia.

"That's right. I figured it would come in handy at some point. There's no more effective facade than one that presents you as a different gender," I answered.

I'd thought about disguising Tarte and Dia as boys, but no matter how convincing their appearance was, it would have been impossible for them to act masculine. There was a high chance people would be suspicious, so I had decided against it.

My behavior, on the other hand, was effortlessly feminine.

"...You're pulling this off so perfectly you're making me wonder if this is a long-held fetish of yours," accused Dia.

"That reminds me, Lord Lugh used to wear girl clothes all the time!" exclaimed Tarte.

"Oh yeah, he was dressed as a girl when we first met!" recalled Dia.

They both looked at me with suspicion.

"Give me a break. My mom forced me to wear those outfits," I protested.

"I know, I know. I'm just teasing, Lugh," said Dia.

"I will accept any hobbies of yours, my lord!" insisted Tarte.

My head hurts.

They were giving me no choice. Once we finished this job, I would have to show them just how manly I was. I needed to regain my honor.

First, I needed to take care of the pressing threat. My plan for doing so was already complete.

Chapter 7 The Assassin Makes Romantic Advances

The three of us entered the capital. We used the gate made especially for nobles.

Those nearby undoubtedly saw us as three noble ladies touring the capital who were totally ignorant of the ways of the world. Our fancy clothes practically screamed that our families were wealthy with new money, but we didn't have a single guard with us.

The royal capital may have had a reputation for being safe, but it was still foolish to walk around unprotected like this. We were also a group of beautiful girls—we stood out tremendously.

Typically, assassins wanted to avoid bringing attention to themselves, but this time, I was purposely standing out for the sake of my objective.

After entering the city, we ate lunch at a restaurant that catered to the nouveau riche and then chatted as we enjoyed sightseeing.

"That meal was so good. It had been a while since I'd eaten in the capital," said Dia.

"It was delicious but also really, really expensive. I could use the money we spent to make an entire week's worth of food," replied Tarte.

Dia had enjoyed everything without a care, but Tarte couldn't get over the price and wasn't able to savor it at all.

I had chosen that restaurant intentionally to fit our performance as three foolish aristocratic ladies from upstart noble families that were prospering financially. It was the kind of eatery known for ripping off tourists. People familiar with the royal capital would never eat there.

Unfortunately, Tarte was as bad an actor as I'd thought she'd be. Her true feelings were breaking through the role she was supposed to be playing.

"I enjoyed it very much. It would be exhausting eating such posh food every day, but it's nice to indulge every once in a while," I stated.

Tarte's and Dia's smiles spasmed a little. They still weren't used to hearing me talk like a woman.

I didn't just change my manner of speaking. In order to complete my disguise, I had also made my tone of voice, gestures, and everything else as feminine as could be. I heard Dia whisper, "It's scary how natural he sounds."

One important detail was that my clothes were noticeably less expensive than my companions'. I'd designed our personas to be close friends, but they were a level richer than I. According to our fake IDs, however, I was from the highest-ranking noble family of the trio.

I gave my character this difficulty to garner sympathy from my target. I had rank but lacked funds. That matched the mark, who was from an aristocratic house but struggled financially. Giving yourself a background similar to your target was a fundamental method of earning compassion.

"I thought it was supposed to be hard to get into the capital, but that was really easy," Dia commented.

"Yeah, we got in with our IDs alone," added Tarte.

"Must I repeat myself? We aren't here as simple tourists. We are nobility. Act the part," I ordered.

The identification I'd procured actually belonged to real people. Many nobles had financial difficulties and wouldn't hesitate to give you an ID in exchange for a bit of cash.

"Also, why do we have to wear such restrictive clothing? It's hard walking around in a dress," Dia complained.

"For goodness' sake, this is the royal capital. We have to look our best, otherwise no one will take us seriously!"

Those were lines I'd written beforehand to demonstrate the vanity my character possessed despite her starved wallet. Not even aristocrats would wear such fancy and fettering attire while going around sightseeing. The only people who would think to dress this way would be country bumpkins visiting the capital.

"That's not the only reason, right?"

I couldn't answer Tarte's question while remaining in character. I decided to use a wind spell called Whisper.

This magic delivered softly spoken words to the ears of the person you were talking to and also delivered their replies to you.

It enabled us to converse with each other under any circumstances without being overheard. Additionally, I'd trained Dia and Tarte to be able to speak while only barely moving their lips.

To other people, it only looked like we were walking in silence.

"I'm planning on slipping into a party being held by the man who is going to testify against me. I'm then going to woo him to get the two of us alone. That's why I'm playing the role of a dumb and excited country noble," I explained.

"...You know, it hurts a little that you chose yourself to play the role of seductress instead of one of us. We're girls, in case you've forgotten," grumbled Dia.

"I'm the most qualified. Also, one of you two hitting on another man is not something I want to see," I responded.

"Ah-ha-ha, that makes me feel better about it," Dia said.

"I'm happy to hear that, too. But the thought of you sacrificing yourself for us and doing...that *to a man*..." Tarte gulped.

"I'll be doing nothing of the sort. The purpose of this disguise is to get him to take me to his room."

"Ah-ha-ha, of course. That's a relief."

Was it my imagination, or did Tarte actually sound disappointed?

I'd spoiled Dia's beauty with her makeup and hid Tarte's large chest to ensure they wouldn't receive sexual advances. That said, they'd be denied entrance to the party if they were outright ugly.

Knowing as much, I'd decided to halve their charms, aiming to make them attractive enough to gain admission but not so lovely that guys would hit on them.

By contrast, I'd made myself as beautiful as possible because I was playing the seductress.

I wonder if I should've done more to make them less enticing.

Tarte was charming and cute even without her chest, and Dia was beautiful even with dirtied skin and freckles. I regretted not doing more to diminish their looks.

"*Parties are costly. He must be a very wealthy noble to be able to hold them so often,*" mused Dia.

"*You would think so, but that's not the case with him. He's actually holding these gatherings in an attempt to* make *money,*" I said.

"*Um, how can he make a profit from parties if they're expensive?*" asked Tarte.

Soirees were a source of headaches for nobles. They were obligated to hold them often, and any sign of stinginess would harm their reputations and make it difficult for them to move up through noble society. It was common for nobles to end up endangering their domains in their pursuit to show off to others.

This explained why Dia and Tarte found it difficult to believe he was holding parties to try to make money.

"To lower-ranking nobles and upstart merchants, attending the parties of noted noble families is a way to gain prestige. Many of them will spend exorbitant amounts of money to secure an invitation. Our target is from a famous noble family that has fallen to ruin. He's struggling financially and is using his house's past glory for profit."

"Wow, I'm not a fan of selling your prestige as an aristocrat, but I'm even more stunned that anyone would think they could buy status with money."

Dia was born a major noble, so she detested that kind of thing.

No matter what size fortune one had, it could not purchase dignity and tradition. That was why upstarts paid for connections to notable houses.

It went without saying that forming a bond with a ruined noble family would only make one a target of scorn in high society, but honor couldn't matter less when it came to the struggle for supremacy among upstarts. They were okay with the status alone.

"*There's one more thing I don't understand. Why is being a girl better for this job?*" asked Tarte.

"Apparently, the rich people attending the target's parties are ordering him to gather beautiful, well-mannered noble ladies, and he's struggling mightily to do so. Bad rumors are spreading about him, which means most aristocrats won't associate with him. The social climbers at his events believe that anything can be bought with money, so nobles are afraid their daughters will be treated like prostitutes if they attend. How do you think our target will react if he finds three beautiful and ignorant girls of high birth here to tour the capital?"

"*...He would want to trick us into attending the party,*" answered Dia.

"*But does he have any idea we are here?*" asked Tarte.

"I've got that covered. The spy I placed in the capital who found this information is also an aristocrat. He's a relative of the owner of the ID

I'm using. I had him tell our target that I slipped out of my home to visit the capital with two friends. As expected, the target took the bait. We're supposed to meet him ten minutes from now."

Preparation was the most essential part of assassination. The killing lasted only an instant, but how much preparation you put in beforehand determined the success or failure of the mission.

I had performed thorough research on the target and thought up every conceivable plan. Just like I always did.

A fountain on the city's east side served as a popular tourist spot. The spy I had placed in the capital had told us to wait there.

I checked my pocket watch to see that it was the appointed time. I expected him to arrive at any moment.

"Ah, hey, Lulu. You got here before us. Are these your friends?"

Lulu was my female name. A pleasant-looking man with neat blond hair waved and ran over to me.

His name was Robert. He was the second son of a viscount. He idolized heroes and was an operative thoroughly devoted to me. The man behind him was the target.

He was the one who hoped to trick three ignorant noble ladies into attending his party so he could show them off to the wealthy attendees.

"It's been a long time, Robert. Sorry about this. I know you're busy with work," I said.

"I'd do anything for you, my cousin. Are those two friends of yours?" inquired Robert.

"Yes, they both wanted to meet you. Their names are Torte and Dira."

"Nice to meet you. I am Torte. Lulu has told me so much about you."

"I'm Dira. It's lovely to finally meet you! I've been so excited to visit the big city."

"It's not every day you see three girls this beautiful in one place!"

Tarte and Dia were calling themselves Torte and Dira, respectively. Those were the names on the identification papers I'd bought.

Robert and I were speaking as cordially as if we really were relatives who hadn't seen each other for ten years. We looked as close as brother and sister.

We were putting on this charade to gain the trust of the mark.

Robert is just as useful as I expected. His acting is natural, and he's smart enough to sense my intentions and keep the conversation going.

I decided we had made a good enough show of being on close terms. It was time to begin my assault.

"Robert, is this man an acquaintance of yours?" I questioned.

"Ah, sorry. He's a friend of mine. He is the prince who is going to invite you into high society. That's what you've always yearned for, right?" Robert said.

"High society? Really?!"

I saw a look of relief in the target's eyes. He'd been seeking an aristocratic lady to meet the demands of the upstarts, and he had finally found one in me.

He was so dazzled by the bait in front of him that he didn't doubt us for a second.

The target opened his mouth to speak.

"I will take it from there. I am Count Grant Frantrude, head of House Frantrude. It would be my honor to have you three at a noble party I am sponsoring tonight," he announced.

At this point, the job was already 70 percent complete.

Okay, time to act like he's deceiving me.

"You're a count? But you're so young! That's amazing. High

society in the royal capital… There will be halls with sparkling chandeliers, beautiful music, and graceful dancing! Ah, sorry. I got carried away. I'm from the country, where nothing shimmers at all. I've always fantasized about that kind of thing," I said.

"No, there's no need to apologize. Seeing you this happy makes coming here to invite you feel worth it. My soiree shall provide all that you seek and more. You are welcome to enjoy it to your heart's content."

"Thank you! See, Torte and Dira, I knew that dressing up was a good idea! A prince just fell for me!" I exclaimed.

Count Frantrude beamed. "I'm a lucky man, getting to meet three such beautiful ladies."

I thought back on the information I had received about the target.

Count Grant Frantrude was in his mid-twenties, but as he said, he had already inherited his house. He was chosen to testify against me because he happened to be in Jombull the day I fought the demon.

That wasn't the only reason, though. He was also a man who would do anything to restore his house to its former glory. As such, the mastermind judged him the perfect candidate who would listen unquestioningly so long as money was promised.

House Frantrude fell to ruin because of the previous Count Frantrude's incompetence. He'd wasted a fortune pursuing his hobby of collecting works of art and then sold his family's land to raise quick funds.

Had he been permitted to continue, House Frantrude surely would have perished. For that reason, the current Count Frantrude decided he needed to kill his father and seize control…and then went through with it.

Afterward, he tried to restore their finances by selling the works of art his father had amassed, but the majority of them were judged to be counterfeit. The young count couldn't so much as pay off the interest on a loan.

He then set his hopes on using the name of House Frantrude to curry favor with the upstarts.

Personally, I didn't look down on his efforts. He had resolve and an ability to get things done, and his actions were well-reasoned.

The method he had chosen was dirty, but the man knew it was his only option. Most importantly, Count Frantrude was keeping his house afloat, and he had decreased the debt. Judging by the results, he was in the right.

"Torte, Dira, please thank him. You want to go to a party in the capital, too, don't you?" I urged.

"Thank you very much," said Tarte.

"Wow, a party in the capital. I'm so happy," Dia added. She sounded a little wooden, but not so much so that it risked exposing us.

Count Frantrude grinned, showing no signs of suspicion. I saw unconcealable ridicule in his eyes.

These upstart country bumpkins have no idea I'm just using them. That was probably what he was thinking.

He was utterly ignorant of what was actually going on.

The easiest kind of person to deceive was one who thought they were duping you. They lowered their guard because they thought themselves superior.

I began to probe Count Frantrude as we made small talk. By doing so, I noticed he was very into my look.

I gazed at him lasciviously. It wasn't surprising that he liked me. I'd had Robert inquire about the count's type before I arrived, and I'd constructed my appearance based on that information. My hair color and style, clothes, way of speaking, gestures, perfume, and the topics of conversation were all to his liking.

He was insecure about being a high-ranking noble poorer

than the upstarts who attended his parties, fostering a pretentious attitude in him. To win sympathy, I played up my constructed background, which was similar.

During our conversation, I used the information I picked up to make minute adjustments to my character, further captivating Count Frantrude.

Talking to him has told me exactly what kind of man he is.

Count Frantrude wanted to be respected. He was ridiculed by his peers and seen as a clown who sold his pride to young social climbers in exchange for their money.

He was working himself to the bone using whatever means necessary to save his house from devastation, but even his kin were put off by his actions. He was suffering alone.

The envy of a noble lady with no knowledge of the world had to make him feel good. My flattery alone obviously pleased him.

I was positive that he would take me to his room with a little more sweet talk. Once there, I would make him into my puppet.

"Please follow me to my carriage, ladies. I will take you to my estate. You three are here as tourists, correct? I'll have us take the scenic route."

"Oh, that sounds wonderful. You're so considerate. Are all men in the capital gentlemen like you? You're like a different species compared with the ones back home."

"Ha-ha-ha, I can't say all men in the capital are like me, but I always treat women with care."

The count was really warming up to me now.

I see: Being told that he is better than others makes him happier than simple praise.

That was probably a result of his insecurity. I decided I would shower him with what he wanted to hear. *"You're so much more graceful than those lowly upstarts. You're a true noble, not just in title."*

I would praise him profusely while degrading the people who caused him so much grief.

"Count Frantrude, could you dance with me at the party? I would love nothing more."

"You're a very assertive lady. I would be glad to."

I was the only one he took by the hand when we stepped into the carriage. He left the other two to his subordinates.

The first step was a success. I had made an excellent first impression, and he took no interest in Tarte and Dia.

We all got in the carriage and were on our way.

This was an interesting situation. We were both liars who thought we were fooling the other person. It wouldn't be much longer now until we reached the conclusion of our mutual deception.

It would be clear which of us was the better liar in less than half a day.

Chapter 8 | The Assassin Dances

Count Frantrude gave us a superb tour of the royal capital. He had a complete knowledge of the city, was a good conversationalist, and was attentive. His behavior was refined. He was a noble through and through.

He was the type that was popular with girls. His biggest problem, however, was the elitism that peeked through occasionally. He was a wealth supremacist, something you saw often among the aristocracy.

Noble girls wouldn't approach him because of his bad reputation, and his pride prohibited him from reaching out to commoners. That left him alone and starved for praise.

Consequently, he was also easy to manipulate. I would have total control over his heart.

"Do you like the royal capital, Lulu?" Count Frantrude asked.

"It's a wonderful place. I would like to live here someday," I answered.

"Then how would you like to move into my place?"

"My, you're such a charmer."

I dodged his question, then blushed and looked at him with adoring eyes. I understood that these kinds of gestures would tug at his heartstrings.

We put our hands together and gazed at each other.

"You're a lovely woman, Lulu. That was a joke, but I fear I may actually come to mean it."

"Oh, I knew you weren't being serious. You're terrible, Count Frantrude."

We both laughed bashfully. An innocent atmosphere reminiscent of a teen romance novel flooded the carriage.

I felt glares weighing on me, and I turned to see Tarte and Dia staring at me coldly.

It's not like I'm doing this for fun. I would rather they not look at me that way.

The carriage continued to head for Count Frantrude's estate.

I was in for a surprise when we reached the manor. I suppose this was what I should have expected from a once-famed noble family.

There weren't many aristocrats who could treat guests with such a lavish mansion in the royal capital. Plenty of families had money to spend, but this place possessed the grandeur of history and tradition.

The structure was the final asset left to House Frantrude. If the count hadn't killed his father and used every method available to him to restore the house, this estate would have fallen into other hands long ago.

I praised the estate profusely. This place was the count's pride as a Frantrude, so complimenting it was as good as complimenting him directly.

"This manor is the very embodiment of House Frantrude's history. I will do whatever it takes to protect it…no matter what people may say of me," he said, his aspirations coming through. He must have gotten overly excited entertaining me.

It was likely that providing false testimony against me was part of his efforts to protect this estate.

"'Whatever it takes'? That sounds dangerous. What do you mean?"

"Ha-ha, I don't want to bore you. Anyway, the party is about to begin. I'll lend you a room, so please use it to rest and freshen up."

"I'll do just that. See you at the party."

I smiled and then made for the chamber Count Frantrude had granted me.

As soon as I entered the room, I began investigating it.

I searched thoroughly for any mechanisms that could pick up our voices and then tapped the walls to see how thick they were. Once I confirmed that no sounds would be overheard, I gave permission to Dia and Tarte to speak as themselves.

Dia spoke up first. "I don't even know what to say about what I just saw. You had him totally wrapped around your finger. I feel worse about myself as a woman..."

"When you act like that, my lord, I think you could win anyone over," Tarte commented.

"...It's all just part of the job," I insisted.

They hadn't really accused me of anything, but I wanted to say that because I saw doubt in their eyes.

"I know that. You just scared me a little. If you were to manipulate a man that easily, then what about...?" Dia trailed off. Before she stopped, she was going to accuse me of performing to get them to like me as well.

I did also have the skill to seduce women. It was much easier than cross-dressing and enticing a man.

"I don't act in front of you two. I want to be with you both forever, and that would be meaningless if I made you like me through acting or some kind of trick. It would be exhausting for me, and it wouldn't last very long. Being able to love each other even after we share our true selves is what gives this meaning. That's the kind of relationship we have, don't you think?"

Had I only required their temporary loyalty, I would've played a version of myself that they would've cared for even more. But a relationship of that sort wasn't real and would inevitably unravel at some point.

"Ah-ha-ha, that's good to hear. I love you as you are now, Lugh," said Dia.

"I love you, too. Hee-hee, being your true self because you want to be with someone forever is such a nice sentiment," Tarte agreed.

"Thank you, you two."

Dia raised an eyebrow. "Why are you thanking us?"

"I didn't have a reason. I just wanted to say it," I answered.

"You're so weird, my lord."

I gave my gratitude because they liked me for who I was…but I was too embarrassed to explain as much.

"All right, the party is about to begin. Come here so I can fix your makeup," I stated.

"Sure thing… Lugh, can you teach me how you do makeup sometime?" Dia requested.

"I would like you to show me as well. You're even more skilled than Mother," said Tarte.

"Sure, I don't mind. It's a useful skill for disguise," I answered.

"Yay! Hmm-hmm-hmm, I can't take you being more beautiful than me!"

So that was the reason. As I saw it, though, Dia was already significantly more lovely than my female disguise.

Suddenly, she sniffed the air around me.

"I've been wondering, is that sweet smell a new Natural You perfume? I don't like it."

"I was curious about that, too. It smells familiar. It's sweet like Lady Dia said, but it's not appealing in the least. Why did you choose this? All of Natural You's perfumes are so nice."

They both criticized the scent rather harshly, but that was to be expected. It didn't have any effect on women, but it had a massive one on men.

"I chose it because it's best for the job, of course. You know how Tarte discharges pheromones that attract men as a side effect of Beastification? I harvested them to create this perfume. It's an unpleasant smell for women, but it arouses passion in men."

The pheromones Tarte released when using Beastification were intense enough to mess with the mind of an assassin with perfect control over his mental faculties. I could have employed a variety of aphrodisiacs and love potions, but none were as potent as this. A while back, I'd thought to secure some of Tarte's Beastification scent to use as a raw material, believing I'd find a use for it later.

"You're way too serious about this, Lugh! I can't believe you're going this far to seduce a man!"

"I-I'm so embarrassed. You're wearing my scent… Urrrgggh, you're terrible, my lord."

They were both upset with me for entirely different reasons.

Shoot, I guess I shouldn't have revealed that information.

"Anyway, it's time for the party. Let's get going."

I cut off the conversation with an awkward smile, and we headed for the venue.

A few hours later, the party was in full swing.

I was exhausted, even with Rapid Recovery. The attendees were awful. Every single person there was an upstart who thought they could buy anything under the sun with money and made no effort to hide it.

Obviously, not all people who came into new money were of poor character. I just had a problem with the type who attended parties like this, thinking they could purchase honor and dignity.

Probably because he knew the idiotic clientele didn't know any better, Count Frantrude had cut corners with the party wherever possible. Everything was cheap.

To give some examples, the orchestra providing the background music was second-rate. The food *looked* luxurious, but nothing more. Deep-sea maroru eggs were being passed off as the more decadent caspia eggs. The wine bottles were vintage, but they were filled with cheap alcohol. At a glance, it all appeared high-class, but it was only a charade.

"Urgh, I've never been to such an awful affair," complained Dia.

Perhaps hoping to console her, Tarte said, "Ah-ha-ha, well, we knew what to expect."

The girls were in low spirits and near their limits. They had been receiving vulgar glances and sexually abusive remarks all night, and some men had even demanded that they sleep with them in exchange for money.

I shepherded them to a corner of the hall to give them a break. Then I surveyed the hall and locked eyes with Count Frantrude, who was dealing with his unsavory patrons. He walked toward us.

"Sorry for the wait, Lulu. How about that dance I promised?" he asked.

"It would be my pleasure," I answered.

I signaled with my eyes for Dia and Tarte to wait there, took the count's hand, and made for the center of the hall with him.

"I'm so sorry about tonight. I couldn't have imagined they would behave this vulgarly. I've subjected you and your friends to terrible distress."

"You have nothing to apologize for, Count Frantrude. Those men are at fault. Unlike them, you're a true gentleman. Dancing with you makes my very soul sing."

"It puts me at ease to hear you say that... Those upstart pigs are beyond help. I'm just as bad for having to use them... Ha-ha, sorry. For some reason, being around you causes me to let slip my innermost thoughts and complaints. I've never talked to anyone about this stuff before."

Count Frantrude was a prideful sort and was loath to show any vulnerability. At the same time, he desperately wanted to have someone he could share his grievances with. That was why he revealed his innermost thoughts almost immediately after meeting someone willing to accept him.

My attractive perfume, physical appearance designed to suit his tastes, tone, charming behavior, and the drug I'd mixed into his alcohol all worked together to break down the armor around his heart.

"You're such a strong person," I remarked.

"...Am I? You're the first person to ever tell me that," he admitted.

"It's true. I can tell you have a powerful will. I can't bring myself to dislike someone like that. You may indulge in a bit of wickedness...but it's not easy dirtying your hands to protect what's important to you. I find that admirable."

"I might cry. I think I've always wanted someone to tell me I'm not in the wrong."

Count Frantrude smiled, and we continued to dance. When we separated after the song ended, he looked longingly at my hand and started to say something but was interrupted when one of the pigheaded guests ran up to us. The brute shoved Count Frantrude out of the way, grabbed my hand aggressively, and began to stroke it.

"Dance with me next, girl! Nicely done, Count. Didn't think a senseless loser like you could reel in such a good one! Her hand is so smooth. I knew common girls couldn't compare to the noble variety. This is worth all the money I spent!"

That gave me goose bumps.

Aristocrats always received special treatment. They possessed mana, which actually did give them abilities that surpassed ordinary people.

It was also true that a large number of nobles were attractive. There was a theory some believed that mana, shaped by aristocrats' unconscious desires to be stronger and more beautiful, made it a reality.

It wasn't surprising to learn that a few wealthy commoners took perverse pleasure in making nobles do as they wished. Ruling over those with mana made them feel superior. That was why these upstarts with no titles were hounding the count to snag noblewomen for the party.

"Mr. Chartreux, you're making her uncomfortable. Please act a little more gentlemanly," Count Frantrude chided.

"You sure you should be talking back to me, Count?" the man snarled.

Despite initially trying to stop the man called Chartreux after recognizing my discomfort, Count Frantrude went quiet.

This must be one of his best customers.

I decided to put on a little performance. I needed to make sure this unpleasant experience ended up being worth it.

I started by looking at Count Frantrude and pleading for help in timid silence. He responded by giving me a pleading look of his own.

His message was clear: "*Please dance with this man.*" I performed a momentary look of despair, then gave a resolved nod.

I was playing a maiden willing to sacrifice herself for her love. I silently communicated the message that it would be hard, but I would persevere for his sake.

"I—I would be happy to give you this song, good sir."

"Even your voice is adorable. I'll teach you how to use those hands and hips of yours."

And thus, I was subjected to the dance from hell. His face was too close to mine, he was overly clingy, and he clenched my bottom frequently.

This was the most uncomfortable dance I had ever experienced as Lugh. I had more wretched experiences in my previous life, but this one felt so terrible likely because I now lived as a person rather than a tool.

Evidently, growing to be more human did come with drawbacks.

Thankfully, we got through the party without any major incidents. I can safely declare it to be one of the worst I'd ever suffered.

After I completed my dance with that upstart pig, he pestered me to become his mistress. Continually turning him down proved tiring.

I would have let it slide if that was all he'd done. However, he also cast dirty glances and words at Dia and Tarte.

I couldn't let him get away with that. I was absolutely going to make him pay.

He was unaware of this, but I knew he was the owner of a company that served as one of Natural You's business clients. His enterprise had been about to go bankrupt before it experienced sudden growth thanks to being associated with my cosmetics brand. Almost all of his income depended on his relationship with Natural You.

I could ruin him whenever I felt like it, and Natural You would suffer no damage in the process. There were plenty of replacements.

After the party ended, I had Tarte and Dia go to the room Count Frantrude lent to us.

Count Frantrude had invited me to meet with him alone. The two of us stepped onto his balcony and shared a toast.

"Sorry about earlier. I made you dance with such a terrible man for my own benefit."

The first thing out of his mouth was an apology. He had fallen for me completely. That final act of mine was surely what had clinched it.

"No, I chose not to refuse him. I didn't want to cause trouble for you."

Tears formed in the count's eyes. "…I *will* free myself of this situation. I just need to stick it out for a little longer, and I'll be able to break my ties with their ilk. What I am about to say is for your ears alone. House Frantrude is on the verge of bankruptcy. That's why I have to use those people to raise money. But it won't be much longer until I have enough money to pay off the debt my moronic father is responsible for. Once I get there, I'll never have to cater to those lowlifes ever again."

There was a fire in Count Frantrude's gaze. He was drunk on the alcohol, on the ideal woman I'd created, on Tarte's pheromones, on the drug mixed into his drink, on his newly budding love…and most of all, on me.

"So please stay with me! I need you, Lulu. You're the only person who has ever understood me. You risked yourself for me. I want us to be together."

"Th-this is so sudden. I don't know what to say."

"I don't know what's come over me, either. But I want you more than anything. Once I get the money, I'll be able to keep you safe and make you happy!"

"...I would like a night to think about this. I have a lot to consider."

"Then can you give me your answer tomorrow morning? I will come by your room."

"Yes, I promise to be ready by then. I do have just one thing I want to say first." I paused and kissed Count Frantrude on the cheek. Taken aback, he pressed his hand against the spot.

"I love you. I have from the instant we met. I've never seen a more handsome man in all my life. But we nobles are never permitted to live for our feelings."

I took off running after saying that, ensuring he would never forget me. Placing such obstacles between us would cause his affection and his possessiveness to grow.

He was head over heels for Lulu, which meant her time was at an end.

When the count called on Lulu tomorrow, she would be gone, and Lugh Tuatha Dé would be waiting to use her life as a negotiating chip. With his beloved Lulu on the line, Count Frantrude would definitely betray the mastermind.

Okay, time to return to my room and perform the finishing touches.

My plan was going to ruin whoever dared to plot against me. They were going to pay massively for putting me through this difficult and unpleasant experience.

Chapter 9 | The Assassin Persuades

Count Frantrude's heart was now mine, just as I had planned. My past self likely would have done it easily and without feeling, but I found the experience quite painful.

I was glad for both of our sakes that I succeeded. I wasn't optimistic enough to blindly trust that wooing was guaranteed to work, so I had prepared a backup plan, one far crueler than seduction.

Now as Lugh Tuatha Dé, I waited in the chamber for the count to arrive.

The door swung open, and Count Frantrude burst in. It was poor manners for a dignified noble. He must have been dying to hear Lulu's reply to his question.

"Lulu! Can I have your answer?" he asked with flushed cheeks and hope in his voice. A beautiful bouquet of flowers was clasped in his hands.

"Hate to break it to you, but the girl you've fallen for isn't here," I said coldly, giving him the bad news.

"How did you get into my estate?!"

"I recommend you keep quiet… Anything less might endanger her life."

I walked around the dumbfounded Count Frantrude, closed the door, then nudged him in the back. He staggered, tripped over a chair I had prepared, and then plopped down onto it.

"Who the hell are you?!"

"Huh, I was sure you would know me. I'm the man you're trying to frame."

He was shocked speechless, and then he averted his eyes.

"How?"

"'How,' you say? Are you inquiring about how I learned of this scheme in the royal capital? Or how I am here when I'm supposed to be in the faraway Tuatha Dé domain? Or how I determined you are the one providing false testimony against me? Or maybe you're wondering how I know that you have a budding romance with a girl named Lulu?"

I wanted him to think I knew everything to sway the negotiation in my favor. Obviously, I actually did know pretty much everything.

Count Frantrude's face was pale.

"Let's just talk this through, all right? I'd like to be as civilized as possible. That said, you've really upset me. You should watch your behavior, because I have no idea what I might do."

I tossed him a necklace as I finished speaking. It was one I'd worn as Lulu yesterday. I'd told the count the piece was a memento from my mother to ensure he'd remember it.

"Th-that's Lulu's." He gasped.

"That it is. I took it thinking it would make for a nice negotiating tool," I replied.

"Leave her alone! She has nothing to do with this!"

"That's not entirely true, given her affiliation with you. Her life is now in danger because of the actions of her idiotic lover… Poor girl. I feel bad for her."

"We are not lovers!"

"…You really shouldn't lie to me. My subordinates told me she cried your name when they carried her off. Your agitation is also plain as day."

"I—I will not stray from my ideals for her sake. I killed my own father for House Frantrude. I am willing to cast aside a girl or two, no matter how much I may love them."

Count Frantrude wasn't stupid. The most effective thing to do in a hostage situation was to make the captor believe their prisoner was worthless. Otherwise, the captor would keep trying to leverage their safety against you.

There was just one problem—Count Frantrude was a terrible actor. He had no experience in high-pressure situations like this.

On the other hand, I was more than acclimated to people like him. Persuasion would be a cinch.

"I see. If that's how you want to play it, we can call it here for the day. Tomorrow, I might return with a finger of hers. Oh, right, I'm sure you'd like a sign that she's safe. I'll make her write a letter using the blood dripping from her missing finger. I'll send one a day until she has no fingers left," I stated, whispering the last part into his ear. I filled my voice with malice.

No matter how strong the count was, he wasn't used to dealing with death. This was his first time experiencing the coldness of the world and the malice of a true assassin. It cut through his bluff as though it were made of wet paper.

"W-wait. Is Lulu safe?"

"Yes. Provided you don't try to pull anything, you have my word that I will treat her with care."

"What are you after? What is it you want me to do?"

"Wow, you catch on quick."

I wanted to applaud the count. His teeth were chattering from fear, but he was keeping his head on straight. He could see that I was here to discuss, not kill him, and he took that to mean I wasn't interested in revenge.

He was also right not to attack me or to call for help. He understood that it was impossible to overpower a monster with might comparable to the hero's.

"When it comes time for your testimony at the trial, read this script I prepared. Do that, and I'll return your girl to you."

I casually tossed a note to Count Frantrude. He read it and broke into a cold sweat.

"You're telling me I have to betray Marquis Carnalie. I could never. I owe him everything."

"...Is that so?"

The script said that Marquis Carnalie threatened and bribed Count Frantrude into perjury. Marquis Carnalie was the mastermind behind the plot to frame me.

"This is madness. Marquis Carnalie will never forgive such an affront... He'll seek revenge."

"That won't be a problem. The marquis will be going to prison."

I tossed out another document. It contained information showing where the murder victim had actually died and evidence that Marquis Carnalie had ordered nobles loyal to him to transport the corpse to Jombull.

Honestly, the account was only partially true. The majority of its contents had been fabricated or embellished. I thought most of it was accurate, but it still lacked some necessary details.

Even so, it was adequate to fool a man whose mind was clouded by fear. It would suffice for the moment.

My agents throughout the country were working to gather evidence and complete our case. By the day of the trial, we would have irrefutable proof.

No matter how damning the evidence I presented was, however, it wouldn't be quite enough to corner Marquis Carnalie. I needed Count Frantrude to get me there.

"Wha...? I don't... This is impossible. It's only been a few days since the plan was set in motion. How did you gather all this evidence? How did you get to my estate? It doesn't make any sense!"

"Aren't you aware? I was chosen by the goddess to be a Holy Knight. She appeared in my dreams and told me that people threatened to interfere with my efforts to save the world. When I awoke, I was in the capital."

It was such a blatant lie that it was comical. As far as the count knew, however, the only way to explain the speed at which I'd gathered information and arrived here was to say it was the work of the goddess.

When my Demonkiller spell became public information, I'd explained that the goddess had taught it to me. It was well known among nobles that Lugh Tuatha Dé, Holy Knight, could hear the voice of the divine.

"This is what the goddess said: 'Those who interfere with Lugh's efforts to save the world will cease to receive my blessings.' Are you ready for your life to end?"

"I—I never… I never intended for a second to interfere with saving the world… If I had known the goddess would abandon me, I…"

"Whatever your intentions were doesn't mean a thing. The fact of the matter is the goddess decreed that I would save the world, and you got in my way."

Count Frantrude slid out of his chair.

I think that's enough of the stick.

One of the fundamentals of persuasion was the carrot and stick. The technique involved alternating between negative and positive reinforcement to induce the desired response.

"Look, there's a way you can make it out of this—testify as I tell you to. You can still recover. If you cooperate, you will actually be helping to save the world. The goddess will be pleased with you. She may even bless the rest of your life."

"I will help save the world? But I… I need money. If Marquis Carnalie gets arrested, my family will be ruined."

"If that's all you need, I can provide it. This is all yours if you help me."

I pulled a sack stuffed with gold coins out of my Leather Crane Bag and shoved it into the man's hands.

The Alvanian Kingdom had already begun using paper money, but pieces of gold were still in active use when dealing with other countries, and they were accepted domestically, too.

I chose to use coins because I wanted to gain total dominance over Count Frantrude. People went crazy for the weight, sound, and shininess of gold. Paper wouldn't have had the same effect.

Immediately, the count's eyes lit up. He opened the bag and peered inside.

It was no small sum. Fortunately, now that I had completed the telecommunications network, I could make as much money as I wanted.

"This is so much."

"This is three times what that cheapskate Marquis Carnalie promised you. It's enough to forgive your father's debt. You have no need to cater to those upstarts ever again."

Marquis Carnalie's scheme had a few significant holes. In his rush to advance the plan, he'd been sloppy, leaving behind lots of evidence. However, his biggest mistake was going cheap on the bribery. Paying off his most important witness with a stingy one thousand gold coins was going to be his downfall.

"By the goddess..."

It looked like the carrot was quite effective. One more push was all it would take to break Count Frantrude's mind completely.

I had one more trick up my sleeve.

"Use that money to buy your freedom. Then get your revenge on Marquis Carnalie for deceiving and exploiting you."

"He deceived me? What do you mean?"

"Do you really have no idea?"

I shrugged to feign disbelief.

"You seem to be grateful to Marquis Carnalie for purchasing your works of art and introducing you to the upstarts."

"Th-that's right. If he hadn't purchased all those paintings and sculptures and set me up with those wealthy commoners, House Frantrude would have gone under long ago."

The count genuinely believed he owed everything to Marquis Carnalie. Things could not have been going better for me.

"...There's such a thing as being too trusting, you know. There *were* some counterfeits among the pieces that your father collected. But ninety percent of them were genuine, and the remaining ten percent were so close to the originals that they had real value."

"That's a lie! I hired an inspector to confirm they were fake."

"That inspector was an accomplice of Marquis Carnalie. I have something I think you should see. I drew up a list of the clients Marquis Carnalie sold art to. Galatea's Necklace was sold to Baron Dolaira, Frattora's Vase went to Viscount Marleeda, Faran Furulu's landscape painting was bought by the Balor Company, and the list goes on. Marquis Carnalie fenced every single one for a high price. If you don't believe me, you can confirm it yourself. I'm sure you have an acquaintance or two on this list. Visit their estates and ask to see the art they purchased. They'll be thrilled at the chance to show off their expensive treasures."

"What? Th-this can't be..."

"Your father was a fool, but he had a real eye for finery. His collection was worth more than what he spent to acquire it. If the works had all been sold for the appropriate price, you'd be filthy rich."

Count Frantrude's father had loved art deeply, and he only bought pieces of the utmost quality. He was a disaster as the ruler of a domain, but he was a true expert as a collector. Even the counterfeits he got fooled into purchasing did nothing to diminish his skill of evaluation, given that they were all of higher quality than the originals. He relied not on knowledge but on his heart and his eye for creativity when choosing beautiful pieces.

"Marquis Carnalie is also receiving a commission from the upstarts he introduced you to. The man played you like a fiddle. He's made House Frantrude sell its honor and has profited massively in the process. Are you going to let him get away with this?"

I'd nearly burst out laughing upon discovering all this myself. You didn't see a case of someone being fooled and bled dry to this extent very often.

Count Frantrude was a smart man, but he was naive and overly convinced of his father's foolishness. The marquis had seized upon that.

"Wh-what have I done…? I—I have to make him pay!"

"Here's your chance to do just that. As you can see, I have evidence that pins Marquis Carnalie as the true criminal. All you have to do is provide testimony, and he'll be ruined. Once the trial is over, you can start a new life with this money. With Lulu by your side."

"I can avenge myself…and never have to worry about money again. And Lulu…"

"There's no doubt the goddess will bless you and Lulu for helping to save the world."

"I can be with Lulu…with the goddess watching over us…"

Count Frantrude swallowed audibly and clutched the bag of money tight. He was no longer afraid, and his eyes were trained on the future.

I'd used the carrot and stick, then filled him with a desire for revenge. Count Frantrude was now my puppet, and he would dance as I wished.

My work in the royal capital was complete. It was time to get back to Tuatha Dé.

My operatives throughout the world were busy gathering information to bring down Marquis Carnalie. Come the day of the trial, I would wear an innocent look as I brought down the one trying to destroy me.

He was going to spend the rest of his life in jail regretting trying to mess with me.

Chapter 10 | The Assassin Is Taken to the Capital

I returned to Tuatha Dé, having finished my work in the capital.

Even though I was home, I kept busy using the telecommunications network to collect information. Just yesterday, I'd finally gained enough evidence to complete the documents proving that Marquis Carnalie was the true criminal.

"Just in time..."

Having an instant method of communication was such a massive advantage that it was unfair.

Normally when gathering data from all over, it would take days just to send orders to your on-site agents, and then days again for their reports to arrive. Additionally, new revelations could lead to more targets to investigate and more time waiting for commands and replies to travel. It all involved a lot of delays.

The only reason I was able to put together these documents on such short notice was because I was able to issue orders swiftly.

If one controlled information, they controlled the world. It was no exaggeration to say that I could conquer the planet with this telecommunications network if I wanted to.

"Coming in, Lugh!"

Dia opened the door and walked into my room. Barging into my room without knocking wasn't a case of bad manners; I had an agreement with Dia and Tarte that if my door was unlocked, they were free to come in.

"...That look on your face tells me you created another new spell."

Dia always wore a particular expression when she'd finished crafting some new magic.

"That's right! I really like this one. Here, write it down for me. I can't test it until you do."

Dia proudly explained her new spell.

I'd been too busy lately to help with magic development. As such, I was relying entirely on her.

Earlier, I'd taught Dia a decent amount of knowledge from my previous world that I thought might be useful for magic, and she was doing a superb job of using that to make spells. There were times she even came up with ideas I'd never considered.

Without her help, my magic wouldn't be nearly as diverse.

"That's definitely interesting," I said.

"Your phones and hang gliders made me realize something—magic is useful for more than just battle. Wouldn't this spell be handy?" she replied.

"Yeah, it's great."

Once again, I had to admit that Dia was a genius. This formula was something I'd never have conceived of.

Judging by its function, it was clear she made this for me because I was about to leave for the trial in the royal capital. She was probably too embarrassed to say as much out loud, though.

"*Ahem*, are you prepared for the trial? You'll be branded as a criminal if you lose. You can't let that happen."

"I'm as ready as can be. My evidence is perfect. How the trial goes will depend on how many cards he has up his sleeve that I haven't predicted."

"Do you think it'll be a hard fight?"

"I'll manage. No matter what he has prepared, I'll be able to thoroughly refute his claims."

"That's good to hear. I've been feeling so frustrated, though.

I'm useless in these sorts of situations, and I wasn't very helpful in the capital, either."

Dia gave me an apologetic look, and I shook my head at her.

"That's not true. I was only able to write the formula I used to construct the telecommunications network because of a rule you discovered. You were a great help in the royal capital."

"I don't recall doing anything."

"He jumped at the chance to meet us because of the prospect of inviting three noble ladies to his party. You two also did a great job of serving as my foils."

"What do you mean by that?"

"You know how I gave you both clothes and makeup to intentionally ruin your beauty? I also made sure you didn't fit his taste in women. I did that for two reasons: The first was to protect you, while the second was to ensure that my beauty stood out by comparison. Additionally, I displayed a constant concern and desire to protect you two. Count Frantrude prefers women who look after others, so that earned me his favor. A person's attractiveness is always relative and dependent on emotion. Using other people as a foil to stand out is a common technique."

I'd engineered Dia's and Tarte's appearances so that they wouldn't fit his type and made them rank lower than me in noble society. This created a contrast that emphasized my beauty.

"I don't know if I should be happy or hate you for that! Either way, I want you to keep relying on us. You always seem to go off and do everything yourself when I let you out of my sight."

"Really? I feel like I'm constantly leaning on you."

"Do so even more. I am your older sister, after all."

"You're my younger sister now, though."

"Grr..."

Dia puffed out her cheeks. It was so cute that I just had to smile. She had no idea how big a help she already was to me.

"Ah, looks like they've arrived. Watch over things here while I'm gone," I said.

I looked outside and saw a jet-black carriage parked in front of the estate. That particular style of buggy was only used by government officials sent to meet suspects and transport them to the capital.

"Good luck, Lugh," wished Dia.

I was going to the capital alone. Because I was the accused, I wasn't permitted to bring anyone with me. Dia and Tarte couldn't assist me in the trial anyway.

The moment I got up to go meet the government official, someone came hurrying into my room. It was a breathless Tarte.

"Lord Lugh! I have provisions for the journey!" she announced, thrusting a large basket into my hands.

A sweet aroma wafted from the food within.

"This is bread that will keep for the trip! I baked it because I thought you might not get a proper meal over there. Safe travels, my lord."

Looking in the basket, I saw a long-lasting type of bread that contained different fruits and pickled nuts. I'd taught Tarte this recipe as part of survival training. Evidently, she hadn't forgotten about it.

Perhaps she chose to make this for me in the hope it might help me survive this ordeal.

"Thank you, Tarte. I'll gladly take it."

Truthfully, I'd forgotten that I would need to bring food.

I was being taken to the capital as a suspect. I hadn't yet been convicted, so under normal circumstances, there would be no reason to treat me poorly.

However, there was nothing standard about this predicament. Given Marquis Carnalie's plot to ruin me, he may have bribed the government official to harass me and rob me of my decision-making ability.

Tormenting your opponent, denying them meals, and sapping their willpower were all common tactics to hinder their ability to debate in a trial.

I gratefully stored Tarte's basket in the Leather Crane Bag along with the documents for the court case. I then folded up the Leather Crane Bag, put it into a plastic container I produced with an original spell, and swallowed it.

Thankfully, I could fold the Leather Crane Bag small enough that it fit in the palm of my hand. Had it been larger, this trick would've been far more difficult.

"Uh, Lugh, that bag is really important! Why the heck did you swallow it?!" asked Dia incredulously.

"I swallowed it *because* it's important. With a little practice, it's possible to store things in your stomach and take them out whenever you want. They might confiscate any belongings on my person, so I need to hide it," I explained.

"Do you ever run out of surprises?!"

I also could've easily hidden the Leather Crane Bag in my rectum.

This was a relatively popular technique. Spies regularly concealed communication devices between their butt cheeks, and criminals hid drugs in body cavities to pass through customs.

"You're amazing, my lord… Oh no, I messed up again." Tarte cast her eyes to the floor.

"What's wrong?" I questioned.

"I forgot about your Leather Crane Bag. I should have made softer bread for you instead…"

The panic was plain on Tarte's face. She'd baked me something resembling fruitcake. It was firm and held little moisture so that it would keep for a long period of time.

"It's okay, this is fine. I'm happy to have it. I'll be back in about one week. You'll both be in trouble if you don't finish your homework by then, okay?" Hoping to ease the girls' tension, I cracked a joke.

"Ha-ha, I'll get it all done!" said Dia.

"I will master it before you get back!" promised Tarte.

It would've been a waste to not have them do anything while I was away, so I decided to give them a special assignment.

I was sure they would both grow a lot by the time I returned.

The government official knocked on the door with obvious impatience. Normally, a servant would have greeted him, but this time I did so myself.

"How may I help you?" I asked.

"Is Lugh Tuatha Dé here?!"

The man at the door was middle-aged and slightly shorter than me. He had an overbearing and vulgar manner.

"I am Lugh."

"You should have received a letter a few days ago. I'm taking you to the capital under suspicion for the murder of Count Marlentott."

No such letter had been delivered, of course. They'd tried to catch me unaware by staging an accident that kept the missive from reaching me.

I started shouting in response, saying I never received that kind of letter, I didn't know what he was talking about, and there must have been a mistake. I watched for the man's reaction as I gave my performance.

If he had just been a normal government official, he probably would have found it odd that I never received the letter and then explained the situation to me. However, this man had undoubtedly been bribed…

"You shame yourself, murderer! Follow me now!" he yelled, threatening me by drawing the sword at his hip. A mocking smile spread across his face.

He knew the letter never arrived.

"Okay, I'll go. I can prove my innocence."

He punched me in the face as soon as I said that. I could tell from the blow that he was a mage. That made sense—only someone with mana would be qualified to take a noble in as a suspect.

I had anticipated the strike, and the slowness of his blow made it easy to turn my head to lessen the impact. It looked like a hard strike, but it barely hurt at all.

Despite that, I staggered and fell on my back, then held my cheek in terror.

"They call you a Holy Knight? How pathetic! Don't give me that rebellious look. I don't see any remorse for what you've done! I'm gonna beat it into you by the time we reach the capital!"

He could have his fun for now. I would get him for this later.

After I got into the carriage, my hands were bound, and a blindfold was wrapped around my head. They even gagged me so I wouldn't be able to perform any incantations.

Next, they seized all my belongings, just as I expected they would. All they did was give me a light frisking, though; it could hardly be called thorough.

Two people were assigned to watch me, and it was apparent they were both in the pocket of Marquis Carnalie.

What happened after I entered the carriage was comically predictable. They showered me with verbal abuse, let my meal slip out of their hands and fall on the floor when it was time to eat, and regularly stepped on my feet.

The two government officials were unconscious. Their eyes were open, and their bodies were totally relaxed.

With them in that state, I undid the iron chains binding my hands and removed the gag.

I took out my Leather Crane Bag without difficulty and ate the bread Tarte had made me. It was hard, but the plentiful dried fruits and nuts gave it a luxurious taste.

I was also grateful to find a flask full of warm soup in the basket. The broth calmed my frayed nerves.

"That was delicious. Tarte's grown even more skilled as a cook."

I would have gone hungry if not for her efforts. Now that I had a full stomach, I read over the documents for the trial again.

Meanwhile, the government officials were muttering to themselves creepily. They were motionless except for their twitching fingers.

I'd injected a drug into their necks using needles. These fools weren't skilled enough to locate a weapon hidden on an assassin's person. Plus, binding, blindfolding, and gagging me wasn't nearly enough to keep me from striking their vitals.

The drug was a very strong truth serum I'd prepared. I gave them such a strong dose that it left them unsure of the boundary between fantasy and reality. The amount left a person dreaming with their eyes open, seeing what they wished to.

Judging by their muttering, it seemed like they were both tormenting me in their dreams.

I was a rich noble and the heir to my house. I was good-looking and praised by everyone. As such, both of these two despised me, and they were having the time of their lives beating me up while I was incapable of fighting back.

The advantage of this serum was the realism of the delusions it induced, which lasted for hours. That was why I didn't use a drug that would have simply knocked them out. Their memories of the delusions would remain, and they wouldn't realize what I had done even after they returned to their senses.

I was going to administer the drug regularly until we reached the capital. That would keep them quiet and serve me later on. Regular injections opened one's mind and made them susceptible to suggestion. I was planning on giving them a slightly different kind of chemical the day before we arrived at the capital in order to turn them to my side and gain their cooperation.

"I never really wanted to use this on anyone, though. The aftereffects are nasty."

If they had been simple government officials, I would have behaved during the trip. However, they had been bribed and took delight in tormenting me. I wasn't so kind as to care about the suffering of such people.

"Okay… I've read the documents enough times. I guess I'll work on some magic development."

I hadn't gotten quiet time like this in a while. A little enjoyable research was just what I needed.

I took out a pen and some paper.

Dia had been surprising me with one spell after another lately. I needed to make something that would astonish her.

There was one idea I'd been considering for a while. Dia would surely be delighted when I showed it to her, and then she would build upon it to fashion more new magic.

Chapter 11 | The Assassin Goes to Trial

We arrived in the capital after a few days of travel. I had totally brainwashed the observers and turned them into my loyal servants.

"Nothing to report. He sat there in dejected silence the entire time without any resistance. His possessions have been seized."

That was what I had them say.

The substance I had used to brainwash them was very useful. There were plants in this world that could be fed mana to amplify their medicinal effects as they grew, which meant significantly stronger drugs could be made here than in my previous world.

I appreciated these chemicals, but I took heed of the danger that someone could use them on me as well.

There were nobles who made a fortune on pharmaceuticals. I had knowledge from my previous life and from House Tuatha Dé, which was famed for its medical knowledge, but even then, I doubted I could rival nobles who specialized in the subject. It wouldn't have surprised me at all if they possessed drugs more vicious than what I had.

"...I'm being treated this way even after arriving in the capital."

I sighed at the situation I had wound up in. They had covered my eyes and mouth and restrained my arms and legs even in my jail cell.

This was way overboard for a suspect who hadn't been

convicted yet. Marquis Carnalie had used his influence to ensure I was treated this way. His plan was to cut me off from the world to keep me clueless about the crime he was framing me for and overpower me at the trial.

I had to give him credit for his thoroughness. Still, he had no idea who he was messing with. I had already used my intelligence agents to bribe a number of the prison guards. Those guards let me do as I wished while it was their shift to watch me.

One of the guards told me that the case was tomorrow, exactly as my intel had said.

I decided it was time to slip out of my jail cell for a bit. Those watching me had been bought off by my agents, so I had plenty of time. I would return after obtaining one final weapon for tomorrow's trial.

My trial began the next day in a courthouse in the royal capital.

The hearing was open to the public, so nobles and people qualified to reside in the capital could watch from the spectator seating. This kept the judge and the plaintiff in check, as having witnesses prevented them from performing an unjust trial. This newly introduced system was keeping fraudulent charges down.

Interest was high in my trial because I was a Holy Knight and had already defeated two demons, so the courthouse was packed.

I spotted Nevan in the audience, grinning at me as if nothing were amiss. She must have heard about the case.

She doesn't look worried. Normally, people are finished by the time they're put in this position, though.

Trials weren't held in Alvan unless there was evidence that proved guilt with near certainty. In other words, the verdict was decided the moment a case was approved.

Usually, the plaintiff's evidence would be read and thrust before the defendant, who would be told to confess. If they did so, they would be officially branded a criminal. Even if they didn't, though, the judge had the right to declare the evidence valid and convict them anyway.

Marquis Carnalie himself stepped to the podium as the plaintiff and read his fabricated documents without faltering.

He was stout with a face colored by greed, and he behaved in a haughty manner. He fit the stereotype of a corrupt noble so perfectly that I almost laughed.

I waited for him to finish without interrupting.

"This evidence clearly shows that Lugh Tuatha Dé abused his privileges as the Holy Knight to intentionally kill Count Marlentott, who had been in a feud with House Tuatha Dé. It is an outrage that he would take the rights awarded to him to protect the country's peace and abuse them for his own self-interest! He deserves severe punishment!" proclaimed Marquis Carnalie.

His claim was almost verbatim what my intelligence said it would be.

"The defendant may now speak," announced the judge.

"I did not kill Count Marlentott, and there was never any feud between him and House Tuatha Dé. This accusation is a total lie. A thorough investigation of his evidence should make this apparent," I said.

"You disgrace yourself, Lugh Tuatha Dé. I even have a witness. Count Frantrude happened to be in Jombull at the time, and he saw everything. I have called him here today. Your Honor, permission to have him deliver testimony," the marquis responded.

"Granted. Your witness may take the stand."

Count Frantrude, the man I'd won to my side by cross-dressing, approached the podium.

"I was in Jombull the day the demon attacked, and I happened to catch sight of Lugh Tuatha Dé as he fought. He looked divine as he battled the powerful monsters, utterly devoid of fear. It was captivating. He appeared like a legendary knight out of a fairy tale, and despite the danger to my person, I was rooted to the spot."

Wow, that's a surprise.

It was clear that he wasn't lying. He actually had witnessed my fight against Liogel.

"During the struggle, something diverted his attention from the monsters. He saw Count Marlentott. The count had been knocked off his feet while trying to flee. Lugh Tuatha Dé laughed, then kicked some rubble toward him. The rubble hit Count Marlentott in the head and killed him. I am confident he did it on purpose."

Everyone in the audience began to talk at once.

"That's horrible."

"To think the Holy Knight would do such a thing."

"Sure, he's the Holy Knight, but he's still a lowly baron's son."

I heard many such comments among the uproar.

"Silence!"

The judge struck his podium with his gavel, and silence returned to the courthouse.

"You are sure of this, Count Frantrude?" he asked.

"Yes, it's the truth."

Marquis Carnalie smirked to himself after Count Frantrude finished. He surely thought he had this in the bag.

But he was getting way ahead of himself. He was so intent on setting me up that he didn't realize *I* was the one trapping *him*.

Count Frantrude was not done yet. He took a deep breath, then once again began to speak.

"What I mean to say is it's the truth that Marquis Carnalie threatened me into saying that. He blackmailed and bribed me into giving false testimony. Given that he used me this way, I say it's likely the rest of his evidence is fabricated as well. Your Honor, I am not here today to frame a Holy Knight for a crime but instead to charge Marquis Carnalie for bullying me into committing perjury!"

Marquis Carnalie's face went pale. His earlier confidence had vanished.

The audience grew even louder than before.

Marquis Carnalie hadn't expected for a second that Count Frantrude would betray him. He had been overly confident of the man's cooperation. I, on the other hand, had known about this upset.

It was common for things to go wrong during an assassination or any other operation. Professionals made sure to prepare a plan B or a plan C for such occurrences.

Only an amateur trusted everything would go off without a hitch.

"You fool! Have you lost your mind?!" exclaimed Marquis Carnalie.

"*I'm* the one who's lost my mind?! You're the one pinning a felony on a Holy Knight who risks his life to protect this country, nay, the world. And for what? Repulsive jealousy. I could never do such a thing! You can have your money back. Threaten me all you like. I have decided to abide by my own sense of justice and expose your plan for the good of the kingdom!"

Mentally, I was applauding Count Frantrude. He was giving a convincing performance, and he quickly won over the entire audience. I was the one who had written the script, but it resonated as much as it did because of the actor's skill.

I decided I would increase his reward.

"Your Honor, I don't know what has come over my witness. I ask that you invalidate his testimony," requested Marquis Carnalie.

"I will do no such thing. It does not look to me like he is lying. If what he says is true, Marquis Carnalie, you'll be standing here not as the plaintiff but as the defendant," the judge stated.

"That's absurd. I swear by the goddess, I've done no such thing."

He truly has no shame.

Struggling was going to get him nowhere at this point.

The trial was shifting in my favor. It was time to deliver the final blow.

"Your Honor, may I make my argument? I prepared some documents regarding this case. They contain evidence that Marquis Carnalie has been unjustly plotting my downfall. Please take a look at this summary first," I said.

I had gathered a massive amount of proof, and it would have taken a long time for anyone to read through it all. For that reason, I'd drafted a synopsis and prepared many documents to supplement it.

The judge ordered his aide to collect the papers from me and bring them to him.

Pure shock colored Marquis Carnalie's face. He had ordered for my things to be seized and for any documents found to be destroyed. He was also under the belief that I had been brought here ignorant of the situation and without any time to prepare.

"Good heavens, this says that Count Marlentott wasn't killed in Jombull, but here in the capital, and that Marquis Carnalie ordered his body transported to Jombull after the fact. That's not all—the feud between House Tuatha Dé and Count Marlentott was fabricated, and it was actually Marquis Carnalie who had a hostile relationship with the late count... This is very interesting," commented the judge.

"Lies! It's all lies!" screamed the marquis.

"That is a possibility. But these accounts are far more convincing than the evidence you brought here today. I believe we could use them to prove your guilt. At the very least, I cannot convict Lugh Tuatha Dé here today. Your witness was the only person at the scene of the purported crime. Now that he has retracted his testimony, there is not one person who saw Lugh Tuatha Dé murder Count Marlentott."

"B-but, uh... That's circumstantial evidence!"

"Everything suggests that you are more suspicious than Lugh Tuatha Dé. Marquis Carnalie, do you know what it will mean for you if Lugh Tuatha Dé's documents are verified?"

Falsifying evidence in court was a very serious offense. That alone could result in compulsory labor designed specifically for nobles and the demolition of his house.

To make matters worse for him, he'd tried to try to hinder the person entrusted with saving the country all because of a personal grudge. This was a major crime.

What's more, he was also guilty of killing a noble. Marquis Carnalie was ruined.

"I'm innocent! Who are you going to believe, the head of the honorable House Carnalie or some lowly baron's brat?!" he shouted.

What an imbecile. That statement revealed his hostility toward me for all to see.

It made him look bad in the eyes of the audience. His behavior was enough to convince anyone he'd frame me.

The judge squinted as if he was thinking the same thing.

"To answer your question, I must believe him over you. He has risked his life multiple times to repel the demons. Judging by his achievements alone, he surpasses even the hero as this country's greatest hope. I have reached my verdict. Lugh Tuatha Dé is innocent. Subsequently, I am ordering an investigation into Marquis Carnalie using these documents as a foundation. Depending on the results, a trial will be held to prosecute him. Because I believe there is a high risk he will destroy evidence or flee in order to protect himself, I am exercising my authority as judge to arrest Marquis Carnalie until the inspection is complete," announced the judge.

The door behind the judge opened, and knights entered to restrain Marquis Carnalie.

"Don't be absurd! I'm a marquis! A Carnalie! Why won't you do as I say?! I-I'm innocent!"

He passed by me as he was led away. I used a wind spell to carry sound as he did so. The magic assured that only those I wanted would hear my words.

"Don't think this is over yet. I ransacked your estate while you were away. You've been getting up to some really crooked activities. I'm going to expose it all to the public and end you. I won't stop there, either. Your associates are going down, too. You'll spend the rest of your days in jail wishing you never messed with me."

I filled my voice with malice.

A stain formed on Marquis Carnalie's pants. Someone in the audience noticed it, and whispers spread through the crowd. Before long, people started pointing at him and erupting in laughter.

Marquis Carnalie's face went red, and he trembled from humiliation. For someone as proud as him, there was no greater disgrace.

He had set out to satisfy himself by ruining the impudent son of a baron, but now he was the one ruined beyond saving.

"Lugh Tuatha Dé, I extend my deepest regrets to you. If we can corroborate the information in these documents, we will confiscate Marquis Carnalie's private funds as per regulations and use it to pay you indemnities," said the judge.

"No apology necessary, Your Honor. I'm just grateful you believed me," I responded.

I was glad I got such a levelheaded judge. My greatest fear was that Marquis Carnalie had bought the judge. Had that been the case, it would've been a tough fight.

Bribing a judge was a major offense on its own, however, and would've been very risky.

...If I had been trying to bring someone down the way Marquis Carnalie just was, however, I would have done it. If I used every method of persuasion available to me, it would be hard but possible. Even if the bribery failed, I could just silence the judge before they could tell anyone about it.

In the end, the reason he lost was because he did nothing a small-time villain couldn't do. He wasn't nearly ready to pick a fight with me.

All right, time to test the gift I nabbed for myself.

I'd slipped out of my jail cell yesterday to sneak into his estate. My goal was to find dirt on him for insurance.

Marquis Carnalie had amassed a large collection of valuable goods, all of which had been procured through wicked means similar to how he'd cheated Count Frantrude. Thinking I might find something interesting, I'd cased the estate thoroughly.

I was right to do so. I found a divine treasure that not even my agents knew about.

This was the second divine treasure in my possession. I hoped to study it to learn more about the workings of divine treasures than I could from the Leather Crane Bag alone. Plus, it undoubtedly possessed helpful properties of its own.

Acquiring such a valuable item made the recent hassle worthwhile.

That was why I could find it in my generous heart to forgive Marquis Carnalie. I wasn't interested in fixating on him.

That said, he was going to be tried in court regardless of whether I continued to get involved.

I prayed that he would find it in himself to repent for his misdeeds. He would probably die or attempt suicide before he ever repented...but that was none of my concern.

Chapter 12 | The Assassin Tests a New Divine Treasure

After successfully absolving myself, I was set free after completing a bit of paperwork.

Prison life was too cramped for my liking. Admittedly, though, I could break in and out of a cell of that caliber at will, and it was actually nice to have free time to devote to magic development.

But more importantly…

"Airgetlam… Certainly never expected him to be hiding a divine treasure."

After checking to make sure that no one was around, I took out the divine treasure that I'd pilfered from Marquis Carnalie's vault.

It looked like a silver artificial arm. False limbs weren't all that rare, actually. Airgetlam was special because it was a perfect one that contained a reactor core.

The device was perfect in every sense; it could be attached to anyone's body and function flawlessly as an arm with no sense of discomfort. It reproduced the exact same mobility, flexibility, and sense of touch possessed by a flesh-and-blood arm.

It was also extremely durable, and according to legend, it could even endure a blow from Gáe Bolg, the spear that Setanta had wielded.

The advantages didn't stop there. Mana constantly flowed

from the reactor core. I watched it closely with my Tuatha Dé eyes and saw that the amount of magical energy it outputted rivaled Dia's. In other words, it was on par with the pinnacle of human mages.

I was also surprised to see that Airgetlam's mana changed to match that of its owner's upon contact. That meant its power could be used as your own.

This divine treasure was ridiculously convenient. So much so that I was tempted to cut off one of my own arms and attach it in its place.

"...That would probably make Dia and Tarte sad, though."

I could swap out my right arm for the divine treasure, but I didn't intend to at the moment. I didn't think either of the girls would be happy about me having a magical tool for a limb, even if it did make me stronger. I also wanted to be able to embrace them with my own two hands.

Actually, wait. There were no rules that said I needed to have just two arms or that the artificial arm needed to be attached to my body at all times.

Airgetlam was activated by attaching it to nerves. That meant it could be used in ways beyond a mere arm replacement.

This warranted further investigation.

Before leaving the courthouse, I sneaked into a private room and radically changed my appearance using tools for disguise that I carried around in my Leather Crane Bag.

This case had drawn a tremendous amount of attention, and I would have been bombarded with questions if I left the building as Lugh Tuatha Dé.

Just as I expected, I left the courthouse to find a crowd

searching for me. I cut through the throng and emerged on the other side without anyone realizing who I was.

Nevan wasn't there. She'd smiled at me and left as soon as the trial was resolved. I doubt she came because she was concerned. She likely came to see what I was capable of. I was sure my performance satisfied her.

I handed a letter to an intelligence agent in the crowd. The operative hadn't seen through my disguise, either, but we had agreed on a gesture I could use to show him it was me.

The message was for Maha. I'd written it to thank her for all the help she gave me with this case and to give her an additional request. It also stated that I intended to meet her tomorrow.

She'd been taking on a lot for my sake, and I hadn't given her the proper appreciation. Maha had carried the largest burden during this latest challenge and had undoubtedly worried the most about me.

Maha was the manager of my information network and could see everything that was going on with the case. She couldn't help but speculate as a result.

"It's windy," I said to myself.

A storm was approaching. Judging from the movement of the clouds, the humidity, and the temperature, it would hit in the evening and pass before morning.

Flying during inclement weather would be tough. It wasn't impossible, but it would be exhausting. I wouldn't be able to use Windbreak to nullify the gale because the hang glider required it to fly, and being pelted by the heavy rain would be miserable.

I decided that I would stay at an inn and play with my new toy, then head for Milteu as soon as the storm passed.

Thus, I began to look for an inn in the capital.

The rain had been beating against my window at the inn all night. Just as I predicted, a storm had hit the capital.

I was glad I had decided to wait. I did not want to fly in that storm.

"...It works just as I thought it would."

I analyzed Airgetlam, my new divine treasure, in my room at the inn and learned a few things.

Airgetlam did connect to the body physically, but that was only secondary to the connection via the spiritual path, which concerned the mystical and magical realm rather than science. Given that, I believed it was possible to use it without cutting off an arm.

I attached the arm to a knife and then stabbed it into my shoulder. The blade gouged into my flesh so that I couldn't remove it, and I felt tremendous pain.

Airgetlam's power healed the wound and closed it, and then the arm connected to me physically.

However, it still remained motionless. The reason for that was simple—the spiritual path from my shoulder to my hand was currently only linked to my arm. Airgetlam's connection to the spiritual path was being blocked.

However, I did see it try to link with my Tuatha Dé eyes. By observing the movement of mana, I formed a rough estimation of the formula.

Even now, Airgetlam was searching for a connection to the spiritual path. That made it extremely easy to analyze.

"This looks doable."

I had come across similar formulas during my time researching spells. There were a surprisingly large number of them that utilized the spiritual path. For example, one circulated fire mana through the spiritual path to temporarily cover the body in flame for a powerful, life-risking attack.

A line to the spiritual path could not be secured without cutting off an arm… But I could fix that by creating a new line.

I decided to fashion a spell that would form a branch from the path that traveled from my shoulder to my arm. As I wrote, I couldn't help but think about how much better Dia's version would have been. She was far superior to me where the intricacies of magic were concerned. When I got home, I would have to show her this.

For now, my goal was to get Airgetlam to a usable state. I would be satisfied if I could just get it to move.

I devoted myself fully to magic development. It was rough going, but I felt like I was making gradual progress.

When I finished the spell I desired, I lifted my head to see that morning had come, and the storm had passed. I had been immersed in my work for hours.

"Okay, I'll go ahead and chant it… *Marionette*."

That was the name I had chosen for this new bit of magic. The spell activated, and just as I hoped, the spiritual path from my shoulder branched off. Then Airgetlam, which was still stabbed into my body, found the connection it was searching for. I extended the path and linked to it.

For a moment, I nearly blacked out.

An intense discomfort overcame me. The information load Airgetlam poured into me was enormous, and it was a ceaseless burden on my brain. I was able to handle it because I employed the skill Limitless Growth to increase my mental capacity, but it would have fried anyone else immediately.

Arms contained an enormous amount of information. A human arm had many movable parts, including the fingers, the wrist, the elbow, and the shoulder, and each muscle had to be controlled as well.

Normally, Airgetlam cut into the resources the owner used on their severed natural arm, but because I had forcibly added it on to my shoulder, the data required to move that arm flooded into my brain all at once.

Humans were designed to function with two arms. Controlling three was unnatural, and it was inevitable that there would be complications as my body attempted to process it. It felt wrong and intensely uncomfortable.

Despite that, my strengthened brain somehow adapted.

"…It's connected. Hmm, I could get used to this."

After Airgetlam linked to the spiritual path, the mana created in its reactor core flowed into me. The arm also possessed the ability to strengthen my self-healing and rejuvenate my body.

What's more, I sensed that I could use Airgetlam as a medium through which to release magical power. I could combine it with the power I outputted from my body to double my instantaneous mana discharge.

My instantaneous mana discharge had always been my biggest weakness. Despite my capacity being off the charts, the portion of it that I could release in one go didn't even exceed what an ordinary mage could achieve. This would do a lot to overcome that weakness.

Also…

"I have perfect control over its movement."

I was successfully able to use the artificial arm to draw a concealed knife from an interior pocket and swing it. The movement was smooth and exactly as I intended.

The problem was that I couldn't move my new silver limb without making a conscious effort. For the moment, I wasn't able to influence it on reflex.

Okay, let's figure this out.

Still, there were already many uses for Airgetlam. Hiding it under loose clothing made it perfect for surprise attacks.

For example, I could use it to break through my clothes without warning during a sword fight and swing a blade. No one would be able to react to that. After all, it would never occur to anyone that a person had a third arm.

There were plenty of other fun applications as well. This new divine treasure was a massive advantage that significantly bolstered my capabilities.

"That's good enough for now."

I withdrew the artificial arm from my shoulder. Blood spurted from the deep wound, but it was quickly healed by the effects of Rapid Recovery.

All right, I succeeded in using this divine treasure.

Later, I intended to study it further to deduce how else I might use its technology. Its control was so precise that it could be used as an arm. There was plenty I could learn from it.

"Guess I should get going. It's already morning, and I'm sure Maha is excited to see me."

The sun was rising, and there wasn't a cloud in the sky.

It was a much better time for flying.

I was sure Maha would be angry with me initially for going so long without visiting, but that would quickly turn to joy at seeing me again.

Chapter 13 | The Assassin's Little Sister's Request

I soared through the air and arrived in Milteu. Because I was going to visit Maha, I went as Illig Balor, not Lugh Tuatha Dé.

I approached a spot where one of the communication devices was buried, accessed it with my mobile phone, set it to Dia, Tarte, and Maha's channel, and activated it. I wanted to tell them I was safe.

"This is Lugh. The trial ended successfully in my acquittal. The plan is to spend the day working in Milteu and then return tomorrow."

I was about to end the call there, but someone else accessed the telecommunications network, and voices began to come through.

"Thank goodness you're safe, my lord! I'll have your favorite food ready when you return."

"Why the heck did you take so long to contact us? We were worried sick!"

"Tarte, Dia. I told you both yesterday that he was safe."

"But I couldn't possibly relax until I heard Lord Lugh's voice directly."

"Same here. I pulled an all-nighter waiting for you, Lugh. I've been too worried to even work on spells."

It was Tarte, Dia, and Maha.

Maha had a communication device in her room, but Dia and Tarte couldn't receive transmissions with their phones unless they went to the mountain behind the estate. They must have been so worried about me that they went there yesterday and remained there until hearing from me. I had taught Tarte survival techniques, so they'd likely put up a tent.

"Sorry for worrying you. I have gifts for you both when I get back. Maha, I'll meet you in two to three hours."

"I'm all ready for you here. I adjusted my work schedule so I would have time after the trial. I have all the time in the world for you today, dear brother."

"Aw man, I'm so jealous. I want to go on a date with Lugh, too," said Dia.

"That's rich coming from someone who lives with him," Maha fired back.

"You're right. Sorry, Maha. Hey, do you want to meet up sometime? It's weird that we've never met."

"Yeah, it is. I'll make time in my schedule for you. I have plenty I'd like to talk to you about. We should pick a meeting point."

"We should do this without Lugh, right?"

"Yes, of course."

"Do I want to know what this is about…?" I asked.

Just what were they planning on talking about in my absence?

"There are some things you can't talk about with a guy present."

"There's no need to fear, dear brother. I don't want to fight her or anything. I would never do anything to upset you."

"Yeah, I just want to make friends. Talking like this is already doing a lot to bring us closer."

It sounded like nothing to worry about. That was a relief. I decided I would give them their space for their girl talk.

"I'm hanging up. One thing before I go—everything that is said on this transmission is recorded in the log, so keep that in mind," I announced.

They all seemed to be in a talkative mood, so I thought I should warn them. I didn't think any of them would say problematic stuff, but there was a chance they could let slip something that would be embarrassing for me to hear.

"Yes, my lord. I feel so ashamed I didn't realize I could speak to Maha whenever I wanted."

"You haven't changed one bit, Tarte... But it feels nice to hear your voice."

"Ah, you should come with me, Tarte! Having a mutual friend will make conversation easier."

"I don't know how much help I'll be, but I will do my best to help you two connect!"

That eased my fear a little. Tarte's presence would prevent things from getting *too* weird.

As I walked through Milteu, I was reminded of how lovely a place it was. The city bore the honor of being the largest port in the Alvanian Kingdom. You could find just about anything there.

I picked out a gift for Maha while gathering some things I needed. I'd gotten her some cookies that she liked while I was in the capital, but I decided I would also buy her a bouquet of flowers. Her favorite purple blossoms were in season.

Tarte and Dia didn't care much for flowers. Tarte preferred food, and Dia liked receiving books. Maha had the most traditionally feminine tastes of the three.

After I finished shopping, I went to Natural You's main store.

A friendly receptionist greeted me, and I headed for the room where Maha was waiting.

When I entered, Maha calmly lifted her face from some documents she had been reading intently.

That relaxed demeanor was very like her. Dia or Tarte would have rushed toward me right away.

"I haven't seen you in a while, Maha."

"Yes, it's been a long time. I was so lonely without you."

Maha gave me a strained smile and stood. She had prepared tea for us, just like she always did. Her herbal brews were delicious and relaxing.

"Can you make mine strong this time, please? I brought a gift for you from the capital. They're Marlana raisin cookies. You said you liked these, right?"

"Thank you. Those are my favorite. I used to think goods in the capital were too expensive even if they were high in quality, but now I know the prices are worth it."

I put the flowers I'd bought in a vase as Maha made the tea.

"Meluna flowers, too? I'm not sure how to react to all this attention," she remarked, smiling despite herself.

I was relieved my gifts made her happy.

"I wanted to thank you for the hard work you've done for me."

"I… I'm glad to know you think of me that way. This is actually perfect timing. I want to ask you something."

Maha grabbed the herbal tea and sat in front of me.

"If I can help you, I will. Ask away."

"You're the only one who can do this for me, but let's discuss it after we finish the sweets."

"Sounds good. It would be a waste to let your herbal tea go cold."

Maha paid careful attention to every step of preparation. She put considerable thought into the temperature, the steeping time, the quantity of the tea leaves, and the quality of the water.

There couldn't have been many other people who altered the water depending on the tea leaves they used. There was no concept of hard or soft water in this world, and I hadn't taught her anything about it, either. She'd discovered all of this on her own.

Her tea hit the spot. It was just what my tired body needed.

I broke the seal on the raisin cookies I'd brought, and the scent of grapes wafted through the air. The sweets were a high-quality soft kind. The raisins—the key ingredient—had been pickled in premium brandy, and the spices inserted into the dough brought out their flavor.

They were a luxurious treat with an intricate taste. Maha was overjoyed to have them.

"These cookies really are delicious. I wonder if we could make them, too," she remarked.

"That would be difficult. From what I've heard, they make the brandy exclusively for pickling the raisins. It would be very expensive and require a significant amount of trial and error. Figuring all that out requires a lot of time," I explained.

"You're right. That kind of investment runs counter to our business practices."

"We usually dominate the market either with novel ideas, by utilizing our technological and monetary advantage, or by using our independent distribution network. We don't have much history with taking commonplace goods like cookies and meticulously perfecting them, nor do we have the labor for it. I don't think it's the right course for us."

In business, there were always things beyond your capability.

It was important to focus on what you could do and use that to succeed.

"That's true... But I do want to try this kind of thing sometime as a hobby."

"Natural You has become large enough. If it grew any larger, that would actually give us less freedom. Playing it safe here and opening a shop just for fun might be a good idea."

Natural You was still expanding, and we were in dire need of greater facilities and personnel to keep up with the rate of growth. We were on the verge of becoming so large that we would be unable to monitor every nook and cranny of the company with even the most efficient management.

That came with dangers. We could end up losing control of parts of the enterprise that went unchecked.

Business required the courage and the willingness to pump the brakes.

"I agree with you. I wanted to consult you about that, but you beat me to it."

"I'm surprised to hear you say so."

"Don't insult me. Do you realize how long it's been since you entrusted me with the company, dear Illig? I'll bet I have surpassed you when it comes to skill in enterprise."

"You might be right."

I really was nothing more than an adviser at this point. Natural You had grown to this size because of Maha's ability.

We enjoyed the raisin cookies and herbal tea as we talked about the company, and before we knew it, we had run out of both.

Maha then started to fidget. She did say that she wanted to ask me for something once we were finished eating.

Is her request really so embarrassing?

Maha cleared her throat.

"You know...not too long ago, I realized that something had changed in Tarte. I could tell from her letters that she seemed happy and that she had gained some confidence. She used to always be so timid."

"Huh. Now that I think about it, you're right."

Tarte had always lacked confidence, and that held true even after she became one of the strongest people in Alvan.

But her behavior had been a little different recently. She was acting more self-assured. That much was obvious from the phone conversation earlier. Not too long ago, Tarte never would have spoken that way.

"I asked her why...and she said that you two, uh...did it. Ever since then, I've been unable to stop thinking unpleasant things, like how unfair it is that she got to and I haven't... So, dear brother, could I ask you to do it with me, too? I love you, Illig. I know you think of me as a little sister, and that makes me happy. However, that's not enough for me. I'm afraid that you don't care for me as much as Dia and Tarte and that I'm the girl you think of the least. I'm the only one who's not in a relationship with you, and it hurts."

Maha peered up at me, her face beet-red and her eyes moist.

She looked so cute and innocent.

"...Oh, Maha. Are you really okay with me? The heir of the Balor Company proposed to you... It's such a waste."

I said that in jest, but Maha puffed out her cheeks in response. It was rare to see her do something so childish.

"The Balor Company's power is certainly attractive, but not as much as you... Besides, we could grow Natural You even bigger than the Balor Company if we wanted."

I gave an awkward smile. If any other merchant heard her say that, they would have laughed in her face. But I was confident that Maha and I were up to the task.

"You're right about that… I should warn you, I can't promise to love no one but you."

"I know. I'm okay with it."

Maha got up and sat beside me. She then gazed at me intently.

I think I know what she wants…

So I gave it to her.

"Ngh… Haah. Hee-hee, that kiss was much more daring than your last one."

"That's because I always saw you as family."

"You don't have to stop seeing me that way. But I want to be your girlfriend, too."

Maha kissed me next.

First Tarte and now Maha. I had wound up in relationships with both of them.

I had used techniques from my previous world to win over their hearts and condition them so that they would never betray me. That only affected their loyalty, however, and not romantic feelings.

I didn't use love as part of their behavior modification because it was fickle and ill-suited to creating an everlasting bond. That meant my attachment to Tarte and Maha, and their affection for me, was born from something outside of my design.

I was distrustful of anything that defied reasonable explanation, but the mystery of it did leave me overjoyed.

"Shall we take this somewhere else?" I asked.

"Yes, I already have a place prepared," answered Maha.

"You're always on top of things."

"I'm a merchant to the last."

There was no doubt about that.

We readied ourselves to leave the store. Maha smiled as she led me by the hand.

I was taken by her. She had truly become quite beautiful.

I wanted to make her happy. Initially, I'd acquired Maha because I needed her as a tool. Now, however, I loved her as a precious member of my family.

Chapter 14 | The Assassin Embraces

We disguised ourselves and departed the main store at separate times. I then waited for Maha at the inn she'd made a reservation at.

The place Maha had chosen was extravagant. The furnishings were all nice, and the establishment seemed to emphasize anonymity above all else. This inn protected the privacy of its customers.

Maha and I were both relatively famous, so we needed to take precautions. The representative and the proxy representative of Natural You drew more attention than some lower-ranking nobles. We could pass off walking together as necessary for work, but we couldn't have word spread that we were in a romantic relationship.

Our room had a shower, albeit a primitive one. It was operated by using a foot pump to pressurize a tank of warm water connected to the overhead spout. It was simple, but I was glad to have it nonetheless.

I showered first, and I was now waiting for Maha to come out.

Per her request, I was going to sleep with her as Lugh rather than Illig. She said she wanted to be with the real me.

Maha made no attempt to hurry. She was taking her preparation very seriously.

My heart was throbbing. This luxurious inn was frequented

by couples, and its rooms had a certain atmosphere to them. Above all, this was Maha I was about to sleep with.

"I can't stay calm..."

Just like Tarte had become more adorable over time, Maha had grown to be more beautiful, more so than I ever imagined when we first met.

That was true of Tarte as well. Girls became women before you knew it.

My lack of composure will make Maha anxious. I need to calm down.

Shortly afterward, Maha emerged from the shower. My eyes were drawn to her skin, which was flushed from the hot water.

That wasn't the only thing that caught my eye.

"How do I look?"

"It suits you perfectly."

Maha was wearing dark-blue lingerie that matched her hair. Its alluring design suited Maha's mature persona very well and brought out her attractiveness.

My initial reaction was relief rather than arousal. This was so like her that it made me want to laugh. It was nice to know that even in this situation, Maha was still Maha.

"Come here," I instructed.

"O-okay," she responded hesitantly.

"You don't sound like yourself."

"Yeah, that was kind of like Tarte... I'm really nervous."

Maha started to sit next to me on the bed but decided against it and sat between my legs instead, leaning her body back against mine.

"You smell nice."

"I acquired a special perfume oil and coated myself with it after my shower. I know you like this type of fragrance, and it makes my skin pretty and soft."

"Lingerie and perfume oil? You put a lot of effort into this."

Thorough preparation was Maha's manner in all things.

"I'm not as lovely as Dia or Tarte, so I need to go all out to look presentable in front of you."

"That's not true. They're both attractive, but you're just as pretty as them."

"No, I'm not. Even if you're right, I can't relax unless I dress up. I want to do my best to look nice for you, dear brother."

Her lingerie was at the cutting edge of fashion. Nobles usually had these kinds of undergarments custom-made by famous designers. It couldn't have been easy for Maha to get some. The perfume oil was also very valuable.

It was flattering that she'd gone to such lengths for me. Overcome by her sweetness, I hugged her from behind.

I could hear her heartbeat. Actually, I could hear mine as well. *Ba-dum, ba-dum. Ba-dum, ba-dum.* The sound was evidence of our passion.

"This is really nice," I said.

"Yeah. Word of advice, though: You really shouldn't say things like that to a girl."

"You're back to yourself."

Those kinds of retorts were Maha's specialty.

"Yeah, I feel a lot less nervous now. Feeling your skin on mine is putting me at ease. I've always felt most comfortable at your side… Hey, remember how you used to sleep with me whenever I said I was lonely?"

"Yeah, I do."

Tarte and Maha had both been traumatized from the loss of their families when they were young. They desired the comfort of blood relatives, and I did my best to fill that role for them. Thus, on nights they felt lonely, I had let them sleep in my bed.

"I could never have admitted this then, but there were times when I pretended to be sad just because I wanted to be close to you. I think Tarte did, too… We've both seen you as a man for much, much longer than you think. Did you ever realize that?"

"I didn't. Or more accurately, I didn't want to."

There had been plenty of signs. However, I'd overlooked them because I was set on thinking of Tarte and Maha as family.

"Tarte did a much poorer job of concealing it than me. She would often pleasure herself while in bed with you."

"You did, too, Maha."

"Tarte was a bad influe— Wait, you knew?!" Maha exclaimed, turning around to look at me.

Tarte had been so obvious that I wasn't sure if she'd even tried to hide it, but Maha had attempted to subdue her voice. Maha started doing it a few nights after Tarte did, so she probably thought that if I hadn't noticed Tarte, she could get away with it, too.

"I'm an assassin. I'm always probing my surroundings, even while asleep. Want me to give you the number of times you did it and the exact dates? I have a very good memory."

Maha's face flushed an even deeper red, then she turned forward again as if unable to look at me any longer.

"You didn't have to tell me that. I want to die. What kind of sadistic person notices that and ignores it?"

"I knew you were of the age to have uncontrollable sexual desire, so I let you do as you pleased. It's not such a weird thing to do anyway. I wasn't sure what to think about you using my arm without permission, but…the action itself is good for relieving stress. And by the way, I think you deserve some of the blame for making me worry to the point that I let you sleep in my bed."

"…You didn't do that out of kindness. Urgh, I want to die."

I couldn't see Maha's face, but her ears were scarlet.

"I thought it would be okay to tell you this now, but I guess I shouldn't have?"

"No. I don't want to be the only one feeling this embarrassment, so I'm going to tell Tarte you knew about this later."

Maha, who was usually so levelheaded, was really shaken by this. I could only imagine what Tarte's panic would be like.

"I had heard that girls don't like talking about other girls while in bed, but you seem fine discussing Tarte."

"That's because it's Tarte. She's always been family, and that's not going to change. Also..."

Maha swiveled and pinned me down on the bed. Resisting would have been easy, but I let her do as she wished.

"I'm only getting started with my efforts to make you obsessed with me. I've always been good at studying for a test. I've read many books, and I've used tools to practice. All in the aim of making you happy, dear brother."

"You're a model student, Maha."

"Yes. That's what you wished for, so that's what I became. Leave everything to me tonight... I'm going to make sure you'll never get me out of your head."

Maha smiled and kissed me. She then hung over me and whispered in my ear that she loved me.

Okay, time to test the results of Maha's study.

Her inexperience showed. Research could only get you so far, and she didn't understand that there was much you could only learn from doing the real thing.

Maha became my girlfriend today, but she wanted me to continue being her brother and teacher, too. I would instruct her on the things she needed to know.

I could tell it was going to be a long night.

Chapter 15 | The Assassin Meets the One Who Started It All

I was dreaming.

I was awake, but I knew I was dreaming.

It had been fourteen years since I had last seen this place, formed of scenery that could not exist in reality. It was the white room the goddess had called me to when I died.

"Congraaaaaatulations! You've racked up enough achievement points to grant me more resources to interfere with fate. You won't want to miss the next episode of the goddess's wonderful benevolence!"

Naturally, the owner of the realm, the goddess, was here.

"You haven't changed in fourteen years," I remarked.

"Actually, *you're* the one who hasn't changed. This personality and way of speech were both calculated just for you. You're the only one who gets the privilege of seeing me like this, tee-hee."

It sounded like she'd chosen this personality because it was the best way to communicate with me.

I considered why she would have chosen this temperament for me. This was just a guess, but she might have been acting blatantly suspicious so that I could discern her true motives. Being able to easily understand what she wanted put me at ease.

"More resources to interfere with fate… I see. My encounters with Dia, Tarte, and Maha were way too much of a coincidence. I had been searching for useful allies, but finding one person after

another who fit my criteria was odd. Are you saying you're able to manipulate events like you did in introducing me to those three?"

"Ah, you picked up on that? That's right. I'm so good at influencing the threads of fate that I could do it in my sleep. Those three have helped you a lot, haven't they? They've even serviced you…*in bed*. You're a real lady-killer!"

"…I don't feel great knowing you're responsible for my relationships with them."

"Oh, you have the wrong idea there. It takes an insane amount of resources to exercise control over someone's feelings or actions. Frankly speaking, it would be like nailing jelly to a tree. All I did was change the course of destiny ever so slightly to set you up with the personnel you desired. Arranging the meeting is all I can do, and I have no knowledge of what will happen afterward. You should be proud. You are the reason for violating those three the way you have. Oh no, are you going to assault me next?!"

That was a major relief. I would have felt empty inside if their feelings had been manipulated by the goddess.

"Okay… That's good."

"By the way, today was the day of Maha's death on the original timeline. I'm happy for you. You avoided all of their deaths."

"Are you implying that they all should have died by now?"

"That's right. Let's see, where did I put the Akashic records…? Ah, here they are."

The goddess made a show of producing a very thick book from nothing. *Akashic Records* was written in plain font on the cover.

"According to the original flow of things, Tarte was the first to die. She was abandoned on a snowy mountain so her village would have fewer mouths to feed, and she perished from the cold and starvation while on her way to Tuatha Dé. Dia was next. Viekone was defeated in the war, and she was purchased by a perverted noble who took an interest in her superior magic ability.

He wanted to sire an heir with her, but… Oh, that's disgusting. Humans are so stupid. How could he expect her to have children after doing that to her? She was disposed of after being thoroughly broken. Whew, the poor girl."

It wasn't hard to imagine that happening to those two if I hadn't existed.

"Maha's the last. She was cute, so the villainous director of the orphanage sold her off to a pedophile noble. But you know how tough she is. She won his good graces and became his mistress. She had him wrapped around her finger. Then, just as she was about to open her own store with his backing, a great evil befell her! Crazed with jealousy, the pedophile's wife arranged for Maha to be kidnapped by burglars and…nope. Not reading that. That would destroy my pristine image. She was going to die today."

"You can't have picked three people who would have died if they hadn't met me by coincidence."

There had to be some reason for that. There was clearly meaning behind everything the goddess did.

"You're right. Certain factors make meddling with destiny more difficult. These include an individual's ability and wit and the influence they will have on the future. The greater the person, the more challenging they are to tamper with. However, children who die young have little impact on fate. That means while those three are skilled, their destinies are easy to alter. Talk about getting bang for your buck."

"You're talking like you think of us as pieces on a chess board."

"Of course I do. To be fair, I'm less than a piece myself—a simple prop. As I told you, there is very little I can do."

Her limitations *were* apparent. All she had done over the last fourteen years was introduce me to three girls who should have met their ends.

"That can't be what you called me here to talk about... I have some things I want to ask you. There is too much I don't know about this world. If you really want me to save it, give me information."

I had felt that way ever since meeting Mina, the snake demon. I was way too ignorant of this world. There was no way I could win the game without knowing the rules.

"Oh, come on, that's just mean. You're saying that to hurt me. It would take a *ton* of resources to teach it all. I wouldn't be able to do anything else."

"But it was okay for you to talk my ears off about the girls?"

"Yes, that was no problem. I mean, surely you had already reasoned all that out yourself. That's why it didn't cost anything!"

The goddess's eyes bored right through me, as emotionless as the prop she asserted she was.

She was right. I had conjectured that the goddess had arranged our meetings and that they would have died if we hadn't met.

"Then stop wasting time and tell me what you can. Surely it costs something to call me here. If you're some kind of mechanism, you would never have done that without a reason."

"Ding, ding, ding! Correct! Your achievements have convinced the top brass that the world can be saved, and they have decided to provide some much-needed help. They increased my budget, which I will use to grant you a reward in the near future. That was why I called you here."

"...You can't tell me what it is because that will take resources. So you called me here because this boon is something I would've missed unless you told me about it."

The goddess beamed. Evidently, I was right. It must have been a rather large reward if she wanted to make sure I got it.

"Okay. I'll keep an eye out... I want to save this world, too."

I loved everything I had gained while living as Lugh Tuatha

Dé from the bottom of my heart. I had so many important people in my life, including my parents, who had raised me so adoringly, and Dia, Tarte, and Maha, who had all grown to love me. I didn't want to lose them.

"Then I wish you good luck. You are our only hope left."

"...That sounds like important information. You'd better not have wasted resources saying that."

The goddess had just implied that there had been other people sent to this world besides me, and that they had died. I wondered if she had lied to me at the time of my reincarnation about me being the only reincarnated soul or if I had simply been the first.

"It's fine. I knew you had already picked up on that. Those idiots all stood out because they wanted to cheat their way through life and show everyone else how overpowered they were because of their knowledge from their previous world. But that only succeeded in painting targets on their backs for other humans to kill them. Oh, what a waste they were. At least they died, so their souls could come back to me. Still, I always thought it was best to diversify your investment instead of putting all your eggs in one basket."

Just as she said, I did know of some people who seemed like they may have been reincarnated like me. Each of them had a habit of standing out, and Natural You's information network had found them easily. I had even met some of them directly to ask for their cooperation, but curiously, every one of them rejected me, wishing to work alone.

I was also aware that they had perished. All of the people the goddess reincarnated were highly capable and talented. But human limitations held them back, meaning they could die from the slightest moment of carelessness.

"Okay, we've reached the end of the dream. Make sure to give that adorable Maha a nice morning after. Okay, that marks the end of the goddess's divine message! I'm *pooped.* I'm done with work for the day, so I think I'm gonna head for the spa, then wind down with a television drama and a drink."

The white room began to distort.

Just what was the goddess's reward? I needed to investigate. I couldn't risk missing it.

Chapter 16 | The Assassin Breaks It Off

I woke up to find Maha sleeping beside me. I hadn't seen her face so relaxed since when we lived together. She typically kept up her sharp appearance and never showed any vulnerability, so it was pleasant seeing her like this.

"...Tarte, Dia, and Maha would have died if they hadn't met me. I may have already known that, but that didn't prepare me for hearing it directly."

It was easy to call that fate, but I was no longer a puppet who was satisfied leaving things up to destiny. I was brought to this world to stop Epona from going mad. Looking at Maha's sleeping face, though, I couldn't help but feel I had been reincarnated to save those three.

"Good morning, dear brother."

Maha woke up, rubbing her eyes sleepily. She must have been really tired.

Yesterday, I had let her do as she pleased at first, but I took the lead later on. Just as I'd expected, studying could only teach you so much, and Maha was frustrated by her inability. Being the sore loser that she was, she'd studied my actions fervently so that she could keep up. It was funny to watch.

"Good morning, Maha. Do you feel all right?" I asked.

"No, I don't... You're so mean, Lugh," she responded, glaring at me.

I'd been a little too rough for our first time. She was too lovely, and my passion got the best of me.

"Sorry. I'll make tea."

"No, I'll do that. Giving you tea was always my most important job."

"Oh yeah, I guess it was."

Tarte was the servant and did most of the chores when the three of us had lived together, but Maha always took care of the tea.

Maha got up and headed for the kitchen while wearing some comfortable loungewear. En suite kitchens were a selling point of this particular inn. A normal hotel would never have had one in every room.

A pleasant aroma began to fill the area before long.

I heard a knock from outside, and a basket was inserted through an opening at the bottom of the door. That was the inn's breakfast service. Nice timing.

I went and collected it when Maha brought the tea.

"Let's eat breakfast," she said.

"Yeah, I'm hungry after all that exercise last night," I responded.

"Oh, Lugh, you're normally so cool, but you have a real habit of sounding like an old man sometimes. That's sexual harassment."

An old man, huh…? That hurts a little.

"I'll try to be mindful of that."

"Yes, please do. I want you to be the coolest person I know."

Maha smiled, and I smiled back.

I took a sip of the tea. It was very relaxing. As per usual, Maha had put great care into all aspects of its preparation.

We ate the sandwiches next. They surprised me. I didn't have high expectations, but they were pretty good.

"This is Mareuil bread," I remarked.

"Well spotted. The ingredients are top-notch, too. This inn caters to the upper class," Maha explained.

Mareuil was one of the best bakeries in Milteu, and I'd frequented the establishment when I'd lived here. It even looked like the bread had been made and delivered this morning. I could see why Maha had picked this inn. I needed to remember it.

"Whew, I'm full. I'm going to return to work... Before I do, however, I have something I need to tell you," Maha stated.

She passed me an envelope containing some documents. I quickly looked through them.

"This seems suspicious."

"Yes, very. I'm ordering the intelligence agents on site to perform an additional investigation."

The files Maha gave me detailed some strange happenings in the relatively large town of Bilnore, located to the north of Milteu. The area had been struck by frequent earthquakes, and dozens of people had gone missing over the last month.

That wasn't all, either. A wire in my telecommunications network had been cut—the same kind of wire that Tarte had been unable to so much as scratch after swinging one of my knives as hard as she could while strengthened by mana.

That part of the telecommunications network was constructed in a ring formation, meaning that if the wire was cut on one side, the transmission could just travel in the opposite direction, so that in itself wasn't a big deal. But anything powerful enough to sever it was concerning.

Pairing that with the disappearances, something was clearly going on.

"It's probably a demon, and a smart one, too," I theorized.

"What do you think it's up to?" Maha asked.

"We've just killed two very strong demons in a row, the beetle and the lion. I predicted the demons might be careful this time and try to catch us unawares. From what we know, I think the one behind this might be secretly preparing a massacre that will wipe out the entire town at once. It will then try to produce a Fruit of Life and run before anyone arrives to get in its way," I posited.

Until we had more information, I could only offer conjecture, but I imagined the demon was planning to hollow out the ground below the town in order to sink the entire populace at once. That would cause frequent earthquakes and would explain what happened to the cable. A plan like that would kill everyone in the town simultaneously.

Maha nodded. "You may be right. Judging from the beetle demon case, it takes a few days after everyone dies before the Fruit of Life manifests. It probably thinks that killing everyone in town at once will give it enough time to finish everything before we learn of the incident."

After a typical incident, there'd be an investigation. Then the people who could deal with it would be contacted and sent off to the problem site. Despite everyone's best efforts, each of those steps would inevitably take multiple days.

If my theory was correct, it would be impossible to stop the demon from obtaining the Fruit of Life and escaping… Impossible for anyone but me, that is.

"I'm growing more and more impressed by the telecommunications network every day," Maha commented.

Only I could defy the conventional methods. If anything happened in the Alvanian Kingdom, I would learn of it immediately via telephone and then fly there that day.

Even the demons should have had no idea I was capable of that. That was what enabled me to catch them.

"There's one thing I don't understand," Maha said.

"What is it?" I asked.

"Why are the demons only appearing in Alvan? If they want to avoid a fight, wouldn't it be much safer for them to attack a country without you and the hero? The orc, the beetle, and the lion all struck here. If a demon is actually behind this, that will be four in a row."

"I've been suspicious of that, too. I initially thought the demons were targeting this country to draw out and kill the hero. The orc demon even clearly stated that killing the hero was his goal. This time, though, the demon seems to be using tactics to avoid alerting the hero and me. It doesn't make sense for it to attack another location in the kingdom."

From what I had read in this world's old literature, the demons had never attacked one country continuously like this. That was why neighboring nations were trying to secure agreements to borrow the hero in case of an emergency.

The appearance of the demons and the Demon King was a disaster that occurred every few centuries, so many countries had accumulated knowledge of how to deal with it. Each one had a plan in the event of a demon attack, so it shouldn't have made a difference which nation the demons targeted.

Yet they struck here every time. Something had to have changed. There must have been a reason the demons could only attack the Alvanian Kingdom.

"We don't have enough information to go off of yet. We should do more digging and deal with the immediate problems... Thank you. I can use these documents to put a plan into action."

The fastest way to learn about demons was to ask a demon. Fortunately, I happened to know one.

"That's good to hear. I'm going to shower and return to Natural You. I have an important meeting at noon."

"You're really busy."

"Yes, I am. That's my role. It's very difficult, but I'm proud that I can be of so much help to you," Maha replied before walking into the shower room.

This visit had made me realize all over again what a great girl she was.

It was time that I got back to work as well.

I returned to Tuatha Dé after leaving Milteu.

I had my intelligence agents begin an investigation into the town beset by earthquakes and tried to contact Mina, the snake demon.

I was also settling a variety of other affairs.

"Hello, my lord. You're working hard," said Tarte.

"Didn't take long for you to shut yourself away again," noted Dia.

"Looks like you both are finished with today's training," I said.

Tarte and Dia both nodded. They were making the final adjustments on the homework I gave them when I'd left.

"What are you doing, Lugh?" asked Dia.

"I'm following up with Count Frantrude. He was a big help during the trial."

"Ah, I'd been wondering about that. He fell in love with the girl you at the party. What are you going to do about that?"

"I'm sending him a letter as Lulu. I wrote that she returned safely to her domain and that she wants to see him. I also said that she's going to the capital in two months and they can meet up then."

I wrote the letter with feminine handwriting. That was another assassin skill of mine.

"That's just stalling."

"It'll get the job done. We'll exchange lots of letters over the next two months. In them, I will subtly change her behavior, tastes, and habits so that she'll diverge from the ideal woman

Count Frantrude has in his head. It's a bit of a gamble, but I'm sure his love for her will fade before too long. I'll then meet him in person and put on a performance to end their romance for good."

Count Frantrude would likely fall into despair if Lulu dumped him abruptly. That was why I wanted to stall our meeting and sully his affection for her little by little. In the end, I would ensure he left her.

"That sounds like a lot of effort," Dia commented.

"He served me very well. I want to thank him by giving him the cleanest end to this relationship possible. I want him to be at peace about the breakup and have no lingering feelings."

The human heart was fickle. The love between Lulu and Count Frantrude was dramatic and passionate but ultimately fleeting. He knew very little about her, and upon learning more, he would realize she was not his ideal partner and lose interest.

"That's terrifying, my lord… I would still love you forever no matter how coldly you treated me," stated Tarte.

Dia snickered. "You're such a worrywart, Tarte. Your mind went right to the idea of him doing this to you."

"Um, well, I don't think Lord Lugh would ever abandon me. I just got a little scared."

"It's okay to feel that way, Tarte. It's perfectly natural to be frightened of someone who is able to play with the human heart like I can… I'm only sharing this with you because I trust you both. I believe that you will accept this side of me."

If I was just concerned with ensuring they liked me, I wouldn't show them the nastier things I got up to as an assassin. I revealed this kind of stuff to Dia and Tarte because they had my confidence. Additionally, I knew they were worried about the Lulu matter, and this would help reassure them.

"Okay! You can trust me, my lord."

"If something like that was going to turn me away, I never would have liked you in the first place."

"Really?"

I gave an awkward smile and finished writing the letter. Then I tied it to a carrier pigeon's leg.

This carrier pigeon didn't belong to Tuatha Dé—it was one Count Frantrude had addressed to Lulu. He had no clue that the bird he was using to send presents of love would end up leading to his breakup.

The little pigeon flapped its wings and took off into the sky. I was done with the Count Frantrude matter for now.

I cleared my throat. "Tarte, Dia, you'll both present your homework to me tomorrow. Please be prepared."

Next, it was time to determine how much stronger they had gotten during my absence.

Interlude

I changed into some comfortable clothes and led Dia and Tarte to the mountain behind the Tuatha Dé estate.

We typically used the courtyard or the training grounds for combat practice, but when we needed a wide space or expected major damage to our surroundings, we chose this spot. It was perfect for testing new magic, and our many sessions had turned the once-thick forest into a wasteland.

"Did you both finish your homework?" I inquired.

"I worked really hard so I could surprise you, my lord!" exclaimed Tarte.

"I aced it," answered Dia.

Confidence radiated from both of them.

Tarte and Dia both really enjoyed being praised. Strangely enough, it appeared to make them happiest when I did so as if they were children. Being talked to like that should become embarrassing once you reach a certain age…but that didn't seem to be the case for them.

"Okay, can you go first, Tarte?"

"Yes, my lord."

Tarte clenched her fists and concentrated until her fluffy fox ears and tail popped out.

As always, her fox features made her look adorable. Underlying that adorable appearance, though, was a palpable bloodlust like that of a wild carnivore.

This was her Beastification skill. I'd gained it from the hero's skill My Loyal Knights, and I then passed it on to Tarte. It was Tarte's trump card, giving her explosive physical strength and sharply heightened senses. The downside was that her behavior was affected by the animal instincts she gained.

Tarte had always been unable to deny those impulses. But now…

"I can see it in your eyes. You've maintained your intelligence," I observed.

She was giving off an aggressive aura, but her eyes still looked like Tarte's.

"Yes, my lord. Just as you told me to, I used Beastification as much as I could and fought to calm myself the entire time. It didn't work at first, but I got better at it little by little," she said.

"Let's test it out, then. Use your best spell, Wind Shield."

Wind Shield covered the body in armor made from air. It provided defense, and it could also be released to gain acceleration, meaning it possessed offensive uses as well. I often employed it myself because of its great utility. It was also an original spell and fairly difficult.

"Watch this. *Wind Shield!*"

Tarte's incantation was fluid, owing to how much she'd used the magic, and the spell activated without faltering. Wind rose around Tarte and wrapped around her.

"Perfect… If you can use difficult magic like that during Beastification, you should be able to use most spells."

"I tested that while you were away. Of all the spells you've taught me, there are only two I can't use."

I knew what they were without asking. Of all the original spells I had given Tarte, a pair of them stood out as especially challenging. Even in her regular form, Tarte could only successfully cast them one-third of the time. Not being able to use those properly had more to do with her ability than Beastification.

"Good job, Tarte. That was a harsh assignment."

I hugged her, and she released her wind armor and leaned her body into mine. I patted her on the head.

"Hee-hee, it was tough, but I persevered whenever I thought about how it would help you, my lord."

The homework assignment I had left for Tarte was meant to strengthen her control over Beastification. Until now, every time she used it, she would lose herself to animalistic impulses and rampage blindly. Her vision narrowed, she attacked recklessly, and she could only use the simplest of spells. The skill did a lot to diminish what she was good at.

Beastification increased her strength tremendously, so even with those weaknesses, she was more than powerful enough. But in a battle with a truly mighty opponent, those shortcomings were a risk.

Wildly attacking alone wasn't enough. Tarte also needed the awareness to defend herself, deceive her opponent, and flee if necessary. The stronger an opponent was, the more important strategy became. Having multiple options was essential to forming a varied battle strategy.

Tarte had many ways to attack and defend, including her spear, hidden pistol, and the many spells Dia and I had given her. Without both her raw force and her wits, she would eventually come up against an enemy she couldn't defeat.

That's why I'd instructed her to cast an advanced spell during Beastification as a benchmark.

Accomplishing that was only possible if she maintained consciousness. It was evidence that she had the ability to reason even after triggering Beastification.

"You passed. I'll give you the reward I promised later," I said, pulling apart from our embrace and placing my hands on her shoulders.

"I can't wait!"

The reward Tarte had requested was a little unexpected, but her eyes were shining with anticipation, so I wasn't going to reprimand her for it.

Tarte dispelled Beastification and stepped back. Dia stepped forward in her place.

"My turn. Time to unveil the fruits of my research!"

She looked even more smug than usual. Though in her case, her pompous expression made her look unbelievably cute.

"Don't tell me you actually did it? I thought I was asking the impossible."

"Really?! I had a feeling. It was ridiculously hard!"

Dia puffed out her cheeks. That looked cute, too, making her appear more funny than scary.

"Sorry about that. You really are amazing, Dia."

"That's 'cause I'm your older sister. This is the improved magic bullet."

It was the type of projectile we used in our pistols. When performing the spell Gun Strike, we created the bullets within the barrel and then used an explosive spell to fire them. For our pistols, however, we prepared the rounds beforehand.

The bullet Dia gave me was engraved with magic runes. It was a magic tool crafted using information I'd obtained by analyzing the Leather Crane Bag.

The little thing was imbued with magic.

"Wow, you made a lot of changes to the prototype," I remarked.

"That's because you got a number of things wrong. It was super difficult without the real thing," she responded.

Before I left, I'd given Dia a prototype bullet, a paper

summarizing the results of my research, and the records of my tests with the prototype. As she said, it would have been best to give her the target of my analysis, which was the Leather Crane Bag, but I wouldn't have been able to win the trial without it.

I closely inspected the improved projectile and realized that my theory during my attempt at constructing it had been incorrect.

Geez, that means I never would have been able to finish it.

"I have one question. How did you notice my method was wrong without even having the Leather Crane Bag?" I asked.

Finding errors in my thesis without the object of study should have been impossible.

"That was easy. Certain parts of it felt wrong to me. The rest of it made sense, but those pieces just seemed off. How can I put it...? It was like it stopped sounding like music. I just adjusted things so that they flowed properly," she explained.

"You're a genius..."

I'd thought I knew just how clever Dia was, yet she still managed to surprise me. She had always been better than me at discovering the rules of magic and developing formulas. I possessed knowledge of the concept of programming and had been a wizard-level hacker in my previous life, but she still noticed things I didn't. Her awareness had always been far greater than mine.

It was possible that what I saw as characters, she perceived similarly to how one sensed sound. She had an innate gift that no amount of effort could acquire.

"Mind if I try it?" I asked.

"Go ahead! I can't wait to see your reaction," she answered.

I nodded, then grasped the bullet tightly and chanted a spell. Finally, I loaded it into my pistol and fired. I successfully hit a large boulder located about two hundred meters away. A few seconds later, an explosion within the boulder blew it to smithereens.

"Perfect... The spell imbued in the bullet activated."

"Of course it did. It's amazing, right?"

"Amazing doesn't begin to explain it."

Dia had taken something I had been at a total impasse with and completed it in just one week.

Rounds like these were sure to be incredibly useful.

Magic's biggest weakness was its range. Explosive spells could only reach a few dozen meters away. If you disregarded accuracy completely, they could reach one hundred meters at best.

However, infusing a spell into a projectile enabled us to fire accurately from hundreds of meters away. Being able to cause a magic explosion from inside of something like I had with the boulder was a massive advantage.

This bullet would serve us very well.

"Are you impressed by your older sister?"

"Of course."

"Do you really mean that?"

Dia stepped forward and glanced up at me with a cute smile. I smiled awkwardly, then hugged her and patted her head like I had with Tarte.

"You really enjoy this kind of thing for someone who likes to call herself my older sister."

"This is totally different. I want to be respected and relied upon like an elder sibling, but I also want to be spoiled as your girlfriend."

"I see. Then I'll do just that."

I did respect Dia, and I enjoyed spoiling her, too. Supply and demand were in sync.

"And don't forget my reward. I pulled multiple all-nighters for that!"

"You worked really hard…"

"You're the one who gave me the homework that required it!"

"That's true."

I was truly surprised that she had succeeded.

They're both amazing.

Tarte and Dia had both triumphed over the massive hurdles I'd set before them and gained new strength in the process. I needed to reward them for their hard work.

I needed to keep growing, too. I wanted to continue to make them proud.

Chapter 17 | The Assassin and the Collapsed City

Something had happened in Bilnore, and we needed to hurry there.

"Reports have stopped coming in."

I had given orders to my intelligence agents in the town, which was experiencing frequent earthquakes, to contact me regularly. I'd instructed them to do so because I knew that if contact ever ceased, it would mean something big.

"I wish there was time to gather more information, though..."

I especially regretted that I hadn't been able to get any help from Mina. I did have the minimal insight the Alam Karla had provided us during our visit to the Sanctuary, though. She'd revealed that there were eight demons, and I knew that meant four were still undiscovered.

There was little to go on, but I could still deduce what was going on to an extent. The problem was that all my information was vague and secondhand... Mina would have been able to give me specifics.

I didn't know if it was simple chance that Mina had vanished or if she was intentionally evading me.

"...That gives me two options."

The first was to continue observing and not act until I was sure we could win. The second was to rush to Bilnore now and search for the demon.

Both had their pros and cons. If I kept a distance and gathered data, I could increase our chances of victory. If the demon completed the Fruit of Life before I was ready, however, it would run. The advantage of going to Bilnore immediately was that it would guarantee a chance to halt the completion of the Fruit of Life, but challenging an enemy blindly was perilous.

"I need to make a compromise."

Ultimately, I elected to head for Bilnore. However, I didn't intend to engage the demon right away. My plan was to scout the situation.

I thought that was the best course of action.

As soon as we finished breakfast, I ordered Tarte and Dia to get ready for travel. They both looked surprised, but they nodded and started on their preparations.

Tarte was bringing a magic spear I'd made instead of her usual foldable one, and Dia was bringing a pistol to be safe. As soon as we were ready, we took off into the sky with our hang gliders.

"We don't know what kind of demon this is, right?" asked Dia.

"Yeah, that's why I'm gonna scout first. I want you both to hide somewhere out of sight," I answered.

"Yes, my lord. That is your area of expertise. I hope the demon is weak this time."

Tarte was once again using her own hang glider, so we were speaking through communication devices.

I was going to investigate alone because that was the best way to avoid detection, and it would make running easier in case of emergency. I wasn't necessarily going to fight the demon if it found me; I was keeping in mind the option of running if I didn't see any chance of winning.

"We actually don't even know if it's a demon yet... It would be nice if this turns out to be nothing."

Truthfully, I was wishing that from the bottom of my heart.

I thought back to the lion demon we'd fought recently. If we had fought him without any prior knowledge, we may not have been able to win. It was only our careful preparation that enabled us to beat him. Mina had said that Liogel was the strongest of all the demons, but that did not mean the others were weak.

"Hmm, we're almost there. We just passed over the town of Baruya," said Dia.

"Yeah, our destination should come into view any moment now," I agreed.

I concentrated mana into my Tuatha Dé eyes to strengthen my vision. I was shocked by what I saw.

I did see Bilnore...but there was no way it could be called a town any longer.

"That's horrible. How could anyone do this...?"

"This is unbelievable. The whole place is underground."

Just as Dia said, Bilnore had clearly sunk underground. A large settlement with a population of several thousand had been swallowed completely. It was a tragedy.

The hole was very, very deep. Not even Bilnore's tallest buildings emerged above the earth. As far as I could tell from above, it was over one hundred meters deep.

From the state of its structures, I understood that the town had fallen in an instant. The entire population had likely died immediately.

How cruel.

"Had I learned of this sooner, I might have been able to prevent it," I lamented.

"There's no use dwelling on that. You couldn't stop it, but let's at least be thankful that we're here now," consoled Dia.

"Yeah, you're right."

I only realized what had happened because of my telecommunications network and because I'd ordered my agents to send me regular updates. If not for me, no one would have known about this until much later.

Thanks to that, we had avoided the worst-case scenario.

We landed our hang gliders, and I headed for the mountain of rubble that had been Bilnore alone. I used wind magic to slowly descend into the giant hole.

It smelled terrible. They hadn't started decomposing yet, but the remains of the crushed citizens were scattered everywhere. The one saving grace for the people was that their deaths had been quick.

I did my best to conceal my presence and walked without making a sound. Even then, the odds of being noticed were still very high.

The majority of creatures that lived below the earth were excellent at sensing vibrations. I could avoid making noise, but it was impossible for me to walk on the ground and not cause some amount of fluctuation, and I was afraid those tremors would give me away. I was being careful by using wind magic to cushion my feet, but that was ultimately just to make myself feel better.

"So this is what making a Fruit of Life involves… The souls themselves are being eaten. This is ridiculous."

If I increased the power in my Tuatha Dé eyes to their limit, I could view souls.

Normally, when a person died, their spirit returned to the heavens. Then, as the goddess put it, they were bleached and placed into a new vessel. When I was reincarnated, the bleaching step was intentionally skipped, leaving me with my knowledge and experience.

However, these souls were being tied here, and instead of returning to the heavens, they were steadily dissolving and being sucked into something.

"I had the wrong idea when I fought the beetle demon."

Back then, I'd thought the beetle demon was absorbing the nutrients and mana from the human bodies in the town in order to make a Fruit of Life. It was likely still after a Fruit of Life, but it was not absorbing the nutrients and mana for that purpose. Souls were used to make Fruits of Life, and he'd only been recycling the remains of the citizens to create more tree monsters.

This made me realize anew how much of a harmful presence demons were to humans. Actually, make that the world. Souls usually returned to the heavens after death, meaning the number of them didn't decrease.

However, those spirits dissolved and processed like this would never be able to reincarnate again, causing the existing number to gradually drop. The goddess and whoever else was in charge were likely going through the trouble of reusing souls because producing new ones was difficult.

"That's why Fruits of Life are necessary for the Demon King's revival," I reasoned.

Mana was a power that souls produced, but it was only partially as strong as the soul itself. The force created from exhausting and condensing thousands of souls would be unimaginably huge. That had to be the reason for the Demon King's almighty strength.

Ah, I see. That makes sense.

All this thinking led me to a certain hypothesis about the true nature of the hero's power. The demons I had met had dropped some little hints.

"There's no way the hero could be human."

"The hero's very existence is different."

"Fighting a monster like that is not possible."

Even the demons saw the hero as alien, and that wasn't just due to the hero's strength. It was the difference in their existential foundation.

In other words, humans and demons were creatures with only one soul, but the hero was born with thousands of compressed souls, making them intrinsically the same as the Demon King. If that was true, it explained why the goddess and her superiors could only produce one hero per era. Making multiple ones would exhaust their supply of souls.

Everything connected in my head. The more I thought about it, the more correct my hypothesis seemed.

"Hyuk-hyuk-hyuk-hyuk-hyuk-hyuk-hyuk-hyuk-hyuk!"

A high-pitched laugh interrupted my thoughts. It was an unpleasant sound.

What is that?

"A living thing in my nest, in my nest. Strange, strange. You're living, but you won't get away, away."

I sensed the overflowing, powerful mana and miasma unique to demons.

Countless slimy pink tentacles emerged from the ground. Each one of them was thicker than me. The tentacles opened sweat glands and spewed pink fog, which began to gradually fill the hole.

This was bad. Breathing this vapor would kill me instantly.

"I need to get aboveground right away."

Scouting was important, but my survival was top priority.

Chapter 18 | The Assassin Flees from the Earth Dragon

I was surrounded by countless mucus-covered tentacles, each one resembling a giant earthworm.

The pink fog they were releasing was dangerous. It was dissolving the nearby corpses and the stone edifices of the ruined town. The vapor must have been heavier than air, as it was steadily filling the hole and blocking my paths of escape.

I had ingested many poisons from a young age in order to build up immunities as part of my assassin training, but I couldn't imagine it would be safe for me to inhale a demon's toxin.

I began an incantation, then summoned wind and used it to blow the pink fog away.

"That'll never work, never work! There's no point, no point in resisting me. I'm watching you."

The tentacles lashed out at me as the voice spoke. They were fast.

Each one moved like a whip wielded by a master of the weapon. The point of a whip could exceed the speed of sound, and each of the limbs moved swifter than that as they attacked with complex and coordinated movements.

Their mass was overwhelming, and keeping track of their curving trajectories was difficult.

But not all hope was lost.

"I'll find a way out of this."

I poured mana into my Tuatha Dé eyes and used wind magic in addition to defensive martial arts skills to avoid getting hit. I must have appeared like an acrobat as I dodged the incoming blows.

I threw a knife, and it stabbed into one of the tentacles. The thing was thicker than my body, so piercing it with a knife wasn't going to cause any pain.

This wasn't a normal blade, however. An explosion severed the tentacle entirely and sent it flying.

The knife was a revamped version of a WASP knife that I'd created. The weapon itself didn't burst. Instead, the tip of the blade injected gas into the tentacle, which caused rapid expansion within the target.

It was extremely effective against living organisms. I'd developed it as a toy simply to kill time, but it proved very useful against this opponent.

I hope it felt at least a little pain…

"Yeah, didn't think so."

The demon neither screamed nor faltered, and the remaining tentacles attacked me one after another. Naturally, the one I'd destroyed quickly regenerated.

I clicked my tongue in frustration and used a wind spell to lift myself into the air.

To put it bluntly, there was nothing I could do. I wasn't going to learn anything useful from messing around here—I needed to retreat.

I jumped high and used magic to continue rising. This demon could not have been a worse matchup for us. It would be significantly more difficult to handle than Liogel.

I eventually rose out of reach of the tentacles, but I knew I couldn't let my guard down. It wasn't going to let me escape that easily.

"Hyuk-hyuk-hyuk-hyuk-hyuk-hyuk-hyuk!"

The ground shook as its peculiar high laugh sounded. The ground began to shake violently enough to cause buildings to crumble.

Then the demon appeared. It was humongous and creepy and resembled a reddish-brown caterpillar. Its length easily surpassed one hundred meters.

Those pink tentacles that had been chasing me writhed within its maw. The monstrous creature leaped at me with unbelievable force, despite its enormous frame. It was as big as a skyscraper yet was steadily gaining on me.

Should I use a Fahr Stone to counter it? No, it's too close. I would get caught in the blast.

It felt like a bit of a waste, but I decided to use one of my most powerful attacks.

"Cannon Volley!"

I quickly produced dozens of artillery guns from my Leather Crane Bag and fired them simultaneously. Normally, I would spike the cannons into the ground to prevent them from being knocked back by the recoil. I used magnetism to try to keep them in place this time, but my mana was unable to fully negate the kick of so many heavy shots at once.

The backfire caused the cannons to blast upward through the air, but the shots still flew in the desired direction. Admittedly, I'd shot with minimal accuracy, but the demon's massive size meant I needed only to aim down.

Cannonballs rained down on the demon, each one piercing its body.

"Hyuk-hyuk-hyuk-hyuk."

It continued its charge unbothered. Its wounds wriggled, and tentacles like the ones in the demon's mouth grew out of each one. It was a repulsive sight.

My attack didn't do any damage, but the overpowering kinetic energy of it slowed my enemy. I thought that would be enough for me to escape.

However, the farthest-reaching tentacles birthed thinner ones that reached upward and wrapped around my legs. The appendages dripped with mucus, and even my special combat clothes made with monster membranes began to melt. If I had been wearing ordinary garments, they would have dissolved immediately, and my legs would have liquefied down to the bone.

I dispelled the wind armor around my body and used it to rocket upward. The explosive acceleration tore the tentacles grasping my legs right off the demon.

I finally managed to crawl out of the hole and onto the surface. I looked back into the crater just in time to see the brown caterpillar shoot out of it and fling itself into the air. It resembled a breaching whale before it fell back down.

"Hyuk-hyuk-hyuk-hyuk-hyuk. Too bad, too bad. Please come again. I must return, return."

A few seconds later, the gigantic demon collided with the ground, causing the earth to cry and shake.

Then it went shockingly silent. The demon apparently killed all who entered its lair but left anyone beyond alone.

I peered into the darkness below and saw that it had already disappeared underground.

"This is really bad. I have a big disadvantage against this demon."

That was being kind. I couldn't think of a single way to defeat it with my present capabilities.

I carefully unraveled the thin tentacles wrapped around my legs and bottled them. There was a good chance that studying them might reveal something useful.

◇

I decided against going back into the hole and instead joined up with Tarte and Dia. I would have been discovered immediately if I went after the demon, and there was no point trying to fight it right now anyway. I couldn't defeat it, and engaging wouldn't teach me anything more, either.

"I'm back," I announced.

"That thing is unbelievably big. We could see it from here," said Dia.

Tarte offered me a glass. "Welcome back, my lord. Here's some lemonade for you."

"Thank you."

I took the lemonade and quenched my thirst.

The combination of sweet and sour hit the spot.

"How'd it go? Did you discover a way to defeat it?" Dia inquired.

"Actually...I'm kind of at a loss," I admitted.

I had been able to come up with a decent strategy for each of the demons thus far, but I was drawing a blank on this one.

"Yeah, me too... I mean, it's gigantic. Demonkiller would never work."

"You're right. It's over one hundred meters long, while Demonkiller's range is a few meters at best. We need to find the Crimson Heart, and if it turns out it's in the middle of its body, we'll never reach it."

Demons were difficult to kill because they repeatedly healed if we didn't use a spell called Demonkiller to materialize their Crimson Hearts, which housed their power of existence, and then smash them. Given the caterpillar's enormous size, however, there was a high chance we wouldn't be able to reach the Crimson Heart.

"We can't follow it underground, either," said Tarte.

"Yeah, it can escape whenever it wants by burrowing into the earth. And it's too big to hold in place," I agreed.

Burrowing gave it a huge advantage. Any time we cornered it, the demon could just dig away and regroup. It also worked as a great defense. For example, I considered smoking it out using Fahr Stone explosions like we did with the beetle demon, but that wouldn't have much effect if it was deep below the surface. That ruled out Gungnir, too.

I was also concerned by how it didn't pursue me very far after I left the hole. That was proof that it was prioritizing completing the Fruit of Life over killing me. Undoubtedly, it would flee at the first sign of danger.

"Oh yeah, I wonder which demon that is," said Dia.

"There's only one of the remaining four demons it could be. It looks like a caterpillar, but it must be the dragon," I answered.

"I thought dragons were supposed to be cooler than that," said Tarte.

"...Sure. But only a dragon could be that big."

There were legends of something called an earth dragon. Apparently, one had swallowed an entire town from below once.

"Hmm, is there anything in legend that says how heroes in the past managed to defeat it? There's no way they didn't struggle with the earth dragon, too. There's nothing they could do about it hiding underground," Dia remarked.

"One story has it that the earth dragon ate the hero and returned below the earth, but the hero killed it from within its stomach," I explained.

"We can probably replicate that. Once inside its body, it wouldn't matter if it went underground, and we'd be able to reach the Crimson Heart."

"Yeah... The problem is, it spews poison gas that can melt stone. I'd really rather not get swallowed."

"Darn, we'd be melted in an instant."

We needed to find an edge. I'd hoped that looking to legend for hints would reveal something. At least we knew that this was an earth dragon.

Now that I thought about it, I recalled reading that a previous hero had a rough fight and was ready to accept defeat when a storm suddenly swept over the area and slowed the earth dragon's movement. Perhaps there was something to that.

"...Might as well try it."

"What are you doing with those Fahr Stones, Lugh?" asked Dia.

"I thought I'd harass our opponent a little before giving up," I answered.

This was just an idea, but it was worth the attempt. I could use the bottled tentacles to perform a test.

Retreating would be the smartest option rather than taking any risks. Epona wasn't liable to get here in time, but withdrawing would at least let us request her assistance. I expected she'd be able to beat this demon.

Still, I didn't want to take that gamble. If we didn't stop the demon here, not only would the Demon King be that much closer to reviving, but another town would likely suffer the same fate as this one.

There was always a chance Tuatha Dé, Milteu, or another place with people important to me could be next. That was why I was going to do my best to stop this. This wasn't for justice—I simply wanted to protect those I cared about.

Chapter 19 | The Assassin Searches for a Means of Victory

My first encounter with the earth dragon went pretty roughly. I couldn't find anything that gave me an edge.

It wasn't entirely fruitless, though. First off, I'd discovered that the enemy was the earth dragon from legend. Knowing this, I was reasonably certain it possessed other abilities I had yet to witness but were described in stories.

Secondly, I had collected some of its severed tentacles, which were currently squirming inside my special bottle. More specifically, they were ones that had sprouted from other tentacles.

Those two things alone hardly guaranteed victory, but it was a start.

"Um, why are you filling those Fahr Stones with mana? You have plenty of prepared ones already," said Tarte, looking confused.

"I'm putting different combinations of elements into these. I brought Fahr Stones filled with non-elemental mana to use as rechargeable batteries and others filled with a mix of fire, earth, and wind mana for bombing. These stones are going to serve a different purpose."

A large amount of magic power could be poured into a Fahr Stone, and changing the composition inside altered the Fahr Stone's nature.

"Oh, I see. You're going to cause a storm," observed Dia.

"That's right. Using the wind and water mana of three hundred mages will allow me to cause a storm, which will directly lower the earth dragon's strength. I've never tried this before, but legend has it that rain slowed this demon, so it's worth a shot," I explained, continuing to fill the Fahr Stones with mana.

"Hey, that's an interesting idea. But not even you can prime all those Fahr Stones in such a short amount of time," Dia said.

That would've been true with normal methods. My Rapid Recovery skill only multiplied my mana recovery by a little over a hundred. If I poured magic power into the Fahr Stones with full strength, I would deplete myself before I finished.

"That's why I'm gripping the Fahr Stones filled with non-elemental mana in my right hand to draw power out of them, then converting it within my body and channeling it into empty Fahr Stones. That allows me to fill them without exhausting my strength. I want at least five Fahr Stones capable of summoning a storm."

"I've never even thought of doing that before…but it should work. Want some help?" offered Dia.

"No, I'm good. This is only working because the mana in these Fahr Stones is mine. Your control over magic is elite, but it would be hard even for you to convert someone else's mana."

"That's true… I could do it, but it would take a lot out of me. Sorry."

She had no idea how outrageous even the thought of being able to do that was.

"I have something else I want to ask of you. I'm gonna explain my plan, so listen up. You too, Tarte."

They both approached me and sat down. There was no way I could pull this off alone. I needed both of them.

After gathering my thoughts, I began talking.

"I noticed a number of strange things when I encountered

the earth dragon. You both saw the wormlike tentacles extending from its giant body and its mouth, right?" I asked.

"Yeah, they were big enough for us to see from here," answered Dia.

"I severed one of them using a WASP knife, but it regenerated immediately."

"There's nothing strange about that. Demons always revive endlessly unless you break the Crimson Heart," Dia reminded me.

"Yeah, that's why defeating them has been so difficult," agreed Tarte.

"You're right, but it looked different. While the cut-off part of the tentacle was still in the air, the remaining part that was still attached to its body swelled until the tentacle returned to its original length. What's more, the severed tentacle remained whole."

Dia seemed to catch on, but Tarte looked confused.

"Ah, I get it… That's not very demon-like."

"Sorry, I don't understand."

"A demon's regeneration resembles turning back time. Everything goes back to its original state. That's not how the earth dragon recovered. Its flesh bulged and regrew to create a new limb, while the severed flesh remained separate from its body."

Demons' absurd healing power was their greatest weapon. All the demons I'd defeated previously—the orc, beetle, and lion—had rewound to their original state when injured, and any amputated limbs disappeared almost immediately. The earth dragon's regeneration worked differently, resembling something found in natural creatures.

"So are you saying it's not a demon?" asked Dia.

"No, it was making a Fruit of Life. Only a demon can desecrate souls like that. That means it's a demon. But it may not *all* be a demon."

"...Ah, you think the exterior and interior are different beings."

"Yeah, that's the only way to explain it. The demon is probably in the belly of that beast. That follows with the legend. The notion that the hero killed the demon from within is only half-right. It's likely that the hero encountered the actual demon while inside the earth dragon... Here, I have proof. I didn't realize this during the fight, but bottling up a part of a demon's body like this and taking it with you should be impossible."

I pointed at the tentacles in the bottle, all of which were still jumping around energetically. If the earth dragon was a demon, the severed tentacles would have disappeared.

Things were moving fast when I'd cut off the tentacle with the WASP knife, and it was possible that I overlooked something. This, however, was definitive proof the giant creature wasn't a demon.

I couldn't yet decide for sure that the interior and exterior were separate entities, but if my theory was correct, we had a chance of winning.

"You said you had something to ask of us," stated Dia.

"That's right. If the outside is not a demon, it shouldn't be able to keep up if we deal it enough damage. Unlike the hero, I can't brave the mucus and search inside the earth dragon safely. That's why we're going to kill the external beast to draw the demon out. We should then be able to kill the demon. Here's what I want from you two. When I force the earth dragon out of its burrow, overwhelm it with firepower and kill it for good. Use these to do it."

I gave Tarte and Dia nearly all of the Fahr Stones I had filled with earth, fire, and wind mana to use as bombs.

That left me two big cards to play.

"My job will be to fish the earth dragon from its burrow. No amount of raw strength will kill it if it just dives underground.

Once it emerges from the hole, use all of these to hit it with the biggest blast you can," I instructed.

Dia frowned. "Hmm, how are you going to get that giant thing out of the hole?"

"I'm gonna use the Fahr Stones I'm filling now for that."

This strategy would put me in mortal danger, but I had already confronted the earth dragon once, and my gut was telling me I could pull this off.

"So Lady Dia and I will… Ah, I understand," said Tarte.

"Me too. I'll fill the Fahr Stones beyond their capacity and calculate how to position them for the most effective bombing, and Tarte will use wind to position the stones as I order her to," reasoned Dia.

"Exactly."

Fahr Stone blasts were strong, but the way to get the most effect out of them was to inundate and crush the target.

The force from explosions traveled outward radially. If we used the Fahr Stones without any thought to placement, most of the energy would travel away from the target. We could prevent that by surrounding the target with Fahr Stones and triggering multiple bursts at once. The force would all travel inward, giving no room for escape.

Determining the most effective deployment of the Fahr Stones, quickly filling them past their capacity, and timing the explosions all at once should not be humanly possible. Given Dia's smarts and sense for magic, though, I knew she was up to the task. The problem was Dia wouldn't be able to throw the stones where they needed to go.

That was where Tarte came in. She had trained very hard with her wind magic, and her control was extremely precise. I was sure she would be able to deliver the Fahr Stones to the exact positions Dia indicated.

"That's going to be really hard. I'll have to make three-dimensional calculations the moment it emerges from the hole," said Dia.

Tarte nodded. "That sounds really difficult."

"You'll have only a few seconds, and then Tarte will have to position those stones immediately... This is the hardest thing I've ever asked of either of you."

Tarte and Dia exchanged a look. I understood that what I was asking for was unreasonable. I wouldn't be able to support them, either, as sending the earth dragon flying was going to take all of my attention.

"I'll do it," Dia stated.

"...Me too. Um, Lord Lugh, do you think we can do it?" asked Tarte.

"Yes, of course. I decided that your present capabilities are sufficient," I answered affirmatively.

"Then I'll definitely succeed!"

That reply was very like Tarte.

I wasn't ready yet. I needed to prepare for this operation and think of a backup strategy in case it failed.

My plan was built on a number of assumptions. I needed to bear in mind the possibility that it might not work.

A few hours later, I had all the Fahr Stones I'd prepared for this mission ready to go. I grabbed them, jumped into the hole, and used wind magic to maintain my altitude to an extent.

Before the descent, I'd performed a test on the severed tentacles to determine why storms bothered the earth dragon in the legends. The result turned out to be very simple—the creature was just bad with water. Its reddish-brown skin repelled the liquid, but the tentacle mucus washed away when cleaned.

Mucus was very important to the earth dragon. Everything the secretions touched melted and then evaporated into the pink fog, and it also served defensive purposes, as it was slippery enough for blades to slide off without cutting its flesh.

The creature also had a habit of expelling mucus from its innards when its external coat was rinsed off, suggesting that flooding the earth dragon with water would cause it to dry up and weaken.

Understanding that left me with one course of action.

The Fahr Stones I was holding were not the ones filled with wind and water mana; instead, they contained 100 percent water mana. I filled two of the dangerous little spheres past their capacity and tossed them into the hole.

What would happen if a Fahr Stone filled with the water mana of three hundred mages exploded? The answer turned out to be quite simple.

I watched the result play out in front of me. An incredible waterfall surged into the hole, filling it with violently turbulent water.

Drainage in the crater must have been poor; the water level rose quickly. It was as if the liquid had run up against a dam.

If my hypothesis was incorrect and the entire earth dragon was the demon, it should've been content to stay below. If it died, it would just revive immediately. Nothing was keeping it from waiting for the water to slowly diminish.

However, if the exterior was not a demon but a monster birthed from a demon, it would have to surface. A regular creature would not be able to return from death. I didn't know if it would die from losing all of its mucus or from suffocation, but it would perish eventually.

The earth dragon could not take the third option of leaving. According to Mina, once a demon began making a Fruit of Life, it would break if abandoned for too long.

Surely the demon wouldn't want all of its hard work to go to waste. That meant it only had a single option.

"I hate you, I hate you, I hate you! You're making me so mad, so mad!"

The earth dragon's giant figure leaped out of the hole, which had become a full-fledged pool.

Unlike last time, it was out to kill, not to play. I could feel its bloodlust. Flooding its lair must have upset it.

My hypothesis was correct. Now we had a chance of winning.

It was time to remove its ridiculously large armor and get a look at the real demon.

Chapter 20 | The Assassin Tears Off the Enemy's Armor

I'd used Fahr Stones filled with water mana to submerge the sunken town under a lake, and unable to handle the assault of water, the earth dragon leaped out of the hole.

"I hate water, I hate water, hate, hate, haaaaaate! You will pay, pay, pay!"

Being pursued by a mountainous figure like this earth dragon was nothing if not terrifying. But I wasn't going to look away.

Assassins never neglected even the most trivial pieces of information. They understood that data meant everything for ensuring success and survival.

I used the enhanced vision of my Tuatha Dé eyes to observe it very carefully.

I knew it.

The wounds from Cannon Volley had already healed. However, the earth dragon didn't look identical to before the attack. When I broke through its reddish-brown shell, its inner flesh had swollen to close up the wounds, but the shell did not re-form.

I could still see the enlarged pink tissue closing the injuries. We gave it all that time, but it still hadn't fully mended. More and more, it was apparent that the massive caterpillar beast was not a demon.

"The water must have agitated its wounds."

"Hate, hate, hate, hate!"

Flooding the crater had worked precisely because the earth

dragon was injured. If it hadn't been, it likely would have kept its tentacles within its mouth and curled up so the water would be repelled by its shell. It wouldn't have been bothered by the attack at all.

However, my Cannon Volley blasted off too much of its shell. That enabled a large amount of water to soak through its wounds into its interior, wash away its mucus, and cause great pain. This wasn't my intent when using it, but the Cannon Volley ended up not being a waste.

The enraged earth dragon was closing in. Its eight malice-filled eyes were trained only on me. That was a good sign.

It had been at ease during my first encounter with it, so much so that it had been playing with me. It was extremely difficult to predict the next move of an opponent in that state of mind.

Now that it was furious and set on killing me, it would be much easier to deal with. Anger narrowed one's vision, and intent to kill limited one's choices.

As the earth dragon charged, it extended its spear-like tentacles to block off all paths of escape. Using normal evasion methods, dodging would have been impossible.

"Let's play," I said.

I threw a Fahr Stone. This one was filled with 70 percent wind and 30 percent water. Instead of another waterfall, it unleashed a storm containing heavy rain and an explosive gale.

The earth dragon was flying with unimaginable speed for its gigantic frame, but it was only jumping, meaning it was working against gravity. As a result, the gale visibly slowed it. That wasn't all—water was seeping into its innards, washing out the mucus of its tentacles, and dulling its movement.

"I'm wet, I'm wet, I'm weeeet. Nooooooo, he's escaping!"

I was swimming through the wind, a feat possible because I was using my body to manipulate air resistance. I'd created the storm myself, so I knew the changes in the breeze. I used that to accelerate and dodge the earth dragon and its attacks, then slip under it.

The storm cleared, and then I activated four more Fahr Stones.

"Take this!"

The final Fahr Stones were filled with 70 percent wind and 30 percent fire, a ratio specialized for explosive power. They formed a directional burst that sent the giant earth dragon soaring.

I normally mixed in earth mana to maximize destruction but had left it out this time. This was best if all I wanted to do was knock the target away.

Naturally, using a weapon that powerful in midair sent me rocketing toward the ground. I released all of my wind armor to slow myself down as much as possible, but I was still certain to die instantly if I hit the ground.

I knew that this would happen, so I'd come up with a plan beforehand. I put on a mask to protect my eyes, ears, and mouth, adjusted my posture in midair, and covered my body with mana. I then landed in the water, sending up a big splash.

I'd submerged the town primarily in order to pester the earth dragon; however, I'd also done it to use the water as a cushion.

The impact from hitting the water was still enormous, and despite using mana to defend myself and wearing my special assassin's clothes made for shock resistance, I broke several bones.

I ended up tumbling all the way to the bottom of the crater, but I didn't suffer any major injuries. I kicked off the floor and rose to the surface.

"...Well, I'm still alive."

I looked to the sky as I trod on the surface and took off my mask.

My skin was tingling from the dissolved mucus in the water. It was still harmful even after being diluted to this degree.

I saw fifteen shining Fahr Stones fly toward the earth dragon, which had been launched high into the sky. The little rocks traced odd trajectories as Tarte's wind guided them into place so that the force of their rupturing would be directed inward. They were already ready to burst.

As soon as the Fahr Stones all reached their target coordinates, they exploded.

"Way to go, Dia. That was perfect positioning and timing."

Once again, I covered myself in mana for defense and dove underwater. The blast had come from fifteen Fahr Stones; even deep in the hole, I was in danger of being killed.

The Fahr Stones also contained earth mana, scattering countless deadly iron scraps.

The *boom* and shock of the detonation reached all the way to the bottom of the water. The surface of the liquid evaporated, and the entire lake grew warm. Bits of iron rained down, sending up columns of water.

That's what happens when you trigger fifteen explosions, each containing the mana of three hundred mages, at once. Absurd.

I gasped as I came up for air.

Straining my eyes, I searched for the earth dragon. It seemed that the enormous explosions had caused it to vanish without a trace.

If I was right, and it was indeed not a demon, it wouldn't regenerate, leaving only the true demon. Anything less than a demon wouldn't have survived.

I watched intently. If the earth dragon came back, we'd have no choice but to run.

I poured mana into my Tuatha Dé eyes to make sure I overlooked nothing and also used a wind probing spell.

Something began to happen. It looked like I was watching a bad movie in reverse. Scorched pieces of flesh appeared in the air and gathered together in the shape of a human figure, the burns disappearing in the process.

When the regeneration was finished, a humanoid creature

with shining white skin hung in the air. Its appearance was strange, for it possessed no unevenness or orifices. This made it look like a mannequin.

"It's gone? It's gooooooone! My armor, my armor! WAA-AAAAAAAH!"

The demon's scream sounded more like crying than an angry shout. I had thought it sounded like a young boy, and it looked like I was right.

He was clearly mentally immature. Whiplike appendages extended from his alabaster skin and wrapped around a wall. Then he pulled himself to the ground with them. He was likely thinking of fleeing.

The demon's protective armor was gone. I could now kill him. I felt significantly less mana and miasma coming from his body than I had from Liogel.

"Time for my main profession."

Not letting the slightest chance go to waste, I prepared to assassinate the demon. I also made sure I was ready to support Tarte and Dia if they needed it.

The demon had been totally safe inside his invincible armor, but we'd leveled the playing field. He'd had his fun slaughtering this town, but I would show him what it was like to truly fight to the death.

Chapter 21 | The Assassin Finishes the Job

I had removed the earth dragon armor and forced out the demon's actual body.

The documents in the Sanctuary about each demon tended to be more detailed the more difficult they were for past heroes to defeat. The earth dragon armor had been described in great detail, but there was nothing about the real demon except that he was killed inside of the earth dragon.

I suspected that meant he wasn't very strong. That's why I decided to fight him using our normal tactics: Tarte would confine the demon, Dia would fire Demonkiller at him, and I would deliver the killing blow.

When performing a surprise attack, it was best to be out of sight. The hole the demon had bored into the ground was perfect for that.

"Freeze!"

I chilled the surface of the water so I could stand on it. That was all I needed to fire with precision. I could even hit my mark from within the crater. Given Railgun's extreme firepower, shooting through the ground and piercing the demon was going to be a piece of cake.

I produced my Railgun from the Leather Crane Bag and used a wind probing spell to link the air and my vision. The new version of my probing spell enabled me to aim and fire with Railgun from deep underground.

My role in this assassination was to finish the demon off by sniping him and to help Tarte and Dia fight in the case that the demon was too much for them.

~ Dia & Tarte's Point of View ~

Dia and Tarte poked their heads out from a trench they had dug to protect themselves from the explosion and iron shards. As soon as Tarte threw the Fahr Stones, the pair crouched down in the ditch, and Dia formed a strong magic barrier as a lid. Lugh had instructed Dia to do so because they would have died otherwise.

"So…is the earth dragon dead?" Dia wondered.

"Yes, that giant, gross creature is gone. It looks like the only thing remaining is a small human with shining white skin," answered Tarte.

"Then Lugh was right."

Tarte could also use Lugh's special wind probing spell, allowing her to observe the situation carefully while still remaining safely in the trench. However, because the girl's magic skill and computational abilities were significantly inferior to Lugh's, the range of her scan was limited, and the information she collected had to be simplified so she could process it.

"Your role in Lugh's plan is to hold the demon in place," instructed Dia.

"Yes, my lady," Tarte replied.

"Also, don't forget that he told you to run if things become even a little dicey for you."

"I'll be okay. I've learned how to stay calm no matter the situation."

Tarte grabbed her magic spear, Dia drew her pistol, and they both leaped out of the trench.

Tarte injected a drug into her neck. It only worked for a limited time, but it removed the limiter on the brain and increased one's physical abilities and mana output. The substance also boosted her concentration.

Lugh had ordered her to aim for a brief fight. They didn't yet know this demon's abilities, so it would be suicide to not go all out.

Tarte gripped her spear tight, and Dia added some new parts to the barrel of the pistol she'd drawn from the holster on her thigh.

Dia was wielding a remodeled version of her firearm. It was a size bigger, and it could be fashioned into a bayonet by adding parts to the barrel. Magic runes were engraved on the blade.

"This feels great. It'll make me even stronger."

The bayonet had been added partially to give her a close combat option, but more importantly, the weapon served as a magic wand. It gave spells direction and assisted in gathering mana. Dia could cast just fine without the wand, but having it increased her precision and might.

The drawback of using a wand was that she wouldn't be able to use the pistol for self-defense against nearby assailants. That was why Lugh had thought up a combination tool that could act as both. The added weight pushed the pistol's center of gravity toward the front of the barrel, making it more difficult to handle, but its benefits far outstripped its detriments.

"I'm going after him!" said Tarte.

The faceless demon was trying to flee. He'd decided to abandon completing the Fruit of Life and prioritize survival.

They couldn't afford to let him get away. There was no guarantee he couldn't create his earth dragon armor again. And if he did, another town might fall prey to him. Tarte didn't have a moment to spare.

She activated her most powerful skill, Beastification, and her fox ears and tail emerged. A hostile, carnivorous glint filled her eyes. She also performed the incantation for Wind Shield, covering her body in armor made of air that could be used for defense and speed boosts.

"My homework is paying off."

Not too long ago, Tarte would not have been able to suppress her Beastification instincts, hampering her ability to cast spells. Due to her daily training and the homework Lugh had assigned her, however, she could now cast spells as difficult as Wind Shield without issue.

"Danger, danger, danger, must kill."

The faceless demon lacked eyes, ears, and a nose, but he still turned to face Tarte and reached out his right hand. His sharp fingers hardened and extended toward her with the speed of bullets. Tarte relied on the animal senses and superhuman reflexes from Beastification as she released wind to accelerate, dodged the attack, and sped toward her prey.

The fingers she dodged stabbed into the earth, the dirt beneath each finger transforming into a giant golem. They all pursued Tarte.

It had to be some version of the same ability the demon had employed to create the earth dragon. If Tarte had been struck, she might have become his puppet.

"Too slow!"

Tarte ignored the golems chasing her and hurried forward. She released the rest of her wind to move quicker still, leaving the golems in the dust.

"So fast, so fast."

The faceless demon reached out his left hand. Even with Beastification, Tarte would be unable to evade at this distance. It would have been physically impossible, no matter her reflexes and agility.

So Tarte elected not to dodge it.

"You're mine!"

The girl never faltered, and she succeeded in stabbing the faceless demon before he was able to finish lifting his left hand. If she had hesitated even for a second, she would have been too slow.

The demon was pinned to the ground by the spear. Tarte had thrust it down diagonally to pierce the demon and trap him, and she ran past him after the polearm left her hand.

That wasn't the end, however. She turned around and began to chant a lightning spell that Dia and Lugh had developed.

The spell was called Mighty Storm.

As the name implied, it produced a thundercloud and called down lightning. Using a cloud instead of producing electricity directly enabled a stronger lightning attack for the amount of mana expended.

The spell did have some problems. Namely, it took time for the lightning to strike, and as expected of a bolt from above, it was rather inaccurate. With the demon pinned to the ground and Tarte's spear acting as a lightning rod, however, neither of those would be an issue.

The five golems finally caught up to Tarte and tried to interrupt her incantation. A bullet hole appeared in each of them before they had the chance, however.

The golems were so massive that a measly bullet shouldn't have been able to stop them. However, the mana that had been imbued in the bullets expanded, solidifying their joints and rendering them completely immobile.

The shots had been empowered with earth mana.

"I recommend you don't forget about me," Dia stated before beginning a new intonation.

Tarte cast her a look of thanks, then finally completed her own magic.

"Mighty Storm!"

A violent thunderstorm appeared, and lightning struck. The bolt was absorbed into the spear that pinned the demon. Electricity surged through the mannequin-like creature's body, frying his innards.

He had now been brought to a full stop. Dia finished her spell at that moment. There was only one spell she could be using at a time like this.

"Demonkiller!"

It was the one thing in the world that allowed a regular person to slay a demon. It was so difficult that Lugh and Dia were the only two in the world who could cast it, but Dia performed the incantation effortlessly.

She fired a red bullet of compressed mana from the tip of the bayonet that served as a wand. It hit the faceless demon, a field expanded, and a shining heart mixed with crimson jewels appeared in his abdomen.

That was the demon's core. Until that was destroyed, demons would not just regenerate from injuries, they would also revive endlessly. In other words, destroying the core enabled the normally immortal demons to be killed.

"My heart is so beautiful...," the demon muttered, entranced, as his charred skin was restored. He didn't seem to think he was in danger.

Only the hero could destroy the Crimson Heart without the help of Demonkiller, and even once it was materialized, its hardness surpassed that of all metals in the world. Enormous power was required to smash it, and on top of that, Demonkiller only lasted a few seconds.

The demon understood all of that, and that was why he felt at ease. What the demon didn't know was that an attack capable of ending him was approaching at that very moment.

A second later, a bullet traveling ten times faster than the speed of sound shot out of the ground and pierced the demon's Crimson Heart. After a slight delay, his body fell to pieces, and he disappeared.

The demon did not regenerate again. He probably didn't even have time to process that he was dying.

The absurd speed and force of Railgun brought the fight to an anticlimactic conclusion. Another demon was dead.

"Lord Lugh is amazing. He never misses," said Tarte.

"He says he can see by linking with the wind, but he didn't use his eyes at all. Lugh's a monster," agreed Dia.

Tarte ended Beastification, and her fox ears and tail disappeared. Dia removed the blade of her bayonet and returned the gun to her holster.

The pair then exchanged a high five.

"I'm glad we won… That was the weakest demon we've encountered yet," Tarte remarked.

"He had probably invested most of his power into that giant, gross bug. Normally, that would have made him invincible. I wouldn't have stood a chance against it. The way it could flee underground was totally unfair, too," said Dia.

Tarte nodded. "Yeah, Lord Lugh is truly a genius for coming up with a plan to kill that thing."

"That wasn't the only reason we triumphed. That fight felt easy for you because you've become crazy strong. You can fight a demon as an equal now."

"I owe that all to spending so much time by Lord Lugh's side. I feel like if I'm with him, there's no limit on how strong I can become. You are growing very powerful, too, my lady."

Just as Maha had said, Tarte had changed. It wasn't too long ago that she would have modestly deflected Dia's compliment. It was a positive development.

"You're likely right. Anyway, let's go meet up with Lugh."

"Okay! I can't wait to hear him praise me."

The two girls smiled and ran toward the hole where Bilnore had been. To them, the joy of defeating the demon was significantly outweighed by the joy of being praised, stroked, and embraced by the person they loved.

Epilogue | The Assassin Accepts an Invitation

I used wind magic to observe the state of things aboveground. I had no doubt that Railgun had destroyed the faceless demon's heart, but that didn't mean I was free to relax yet.

I used an earth probing spell in addition to my wind one and thoroughly scanned the area.

"...Everything seems fine."

Now that I was certain the demon was gone, I exhaled and released my concentration.

Just to be safe, I would need to check if the light of the demon statue in the Sanctuary changed to red, just like with the lion demon. This one had pulled an entire town underground—I had to be positive it hadn't gotten away, no matter how unlikely that was.

There was just one problem.

I feel a power rising from below... Looks like it was completed.

I felt a tremendous force beneath the frozen surface of the water. There was an object glowing jade green.

It had formed just before I'd fired Railgun, and I saw all of the remaining souls in the area get sucked down toward it at that moment. I'd even felt like I was in danger myself. Had I not been protected by mana, my spirit might have been stolen, too.

There was only one thing the object could be. It was the item that demons created using ten thousand human souls in order to use as a catalyst for reviving the Demon King, a Fruit of Life.

After the faceless demon's earth dragon armor was destroyed, he'd abandoned the Fruit of Life and tried to flee. However, we had unwittingly aided in completing it by stopping him.

"Thank goodness for my information network. We wouldn't have even made it here to fight otherwise."

Without my agents and our remodeled hang gliders, the Fruit of Life would have formed long before we arrived, and the earth dragon would have disappeared somewhere.

No matter how strong I became, it would be meaningless without ways to locate the enemy and the speed to reach them in time. It wasn't hard to imagine a scenario where I never caught up to this mannequin demon and it managed to revive the Demon King.

"Now, what to do with the Fruit of Life…?"

I broke the ice, then used a wind spell to lift the Fruit of Life out of the water and into the air. It resembled a green jewel, but it pulsed like a living organism. It was beautiful and eerie at the same time.

However, a strong impulse overwhelmed all other thoughts regarding it.

It looks delicious.

I started to drool. I had never felt so hungry in my life. The anticipation of feasts and even starvation paled before it. Every cell in my body was screaming for me to eat it.

I summoned all my willpower to resist. Just touching it would be dangerous, let alone consuming it. However, there was something about this object that was making me lose my mind, despite all my assassin's techniques to control my emotions and act logically.

My hand rejected reason and reached for the Fruit of Life. I responded by drawing a knife and plunging it into my thigh. Blood gushed from the wound, and the intense pain distracted me from the jewel a little. I knew that wouldn't last, though.

I used earth mana on the floating Fruit of Life to enclose it within an aluminum alloy. Strangely enough, a barrier of aluminum mixed with silver trapped mana. Typically, I used that when carrying magic tools around.

After I'd surrounded it with the thick alloy, my hunger lessened significantly. I then stored it in my Leather Crane Bag, and the temptation I felt for the Fruit of Life finally disappeared.

"That was close. One mistake and it would have been in my belly."

If I had eaten an item made for the resurrection of the Demon King that contained ten thousand human souls, I probably would have either exploded or turned into a monster.

I wasn't sure of that, though. Human instincts were very reliable. Putting aside ethics, following your gut feelings almost always resulted in the correct decision. You could eat the majority of things you desired to. You naturally hungered for what your body craved, after all.

If my instincts were telling me to eat the Fruit of Life, there was a chance it would be good for me. I didn't want to take that gamble, though. Losing could mean either dying or becoming a monster.

It was too risky.

Performing human experimentation would also prove difficult. My subject could become a terrifyingly powerful creature the moment I fed the fruit to them.

Still, I could conceive of other uses. Studying the Fruit of Life might reveal more about the Demon King. I could also use it as a negotiating chip with Mina.

Destroying it was also an option.

Regardless, the best thing to do at present was take it with me rather than make a hasty choice. It only delayed the issue, though.

"Guess I should go back aboveground."

I sensed with the wind that Tarte and Dia were racing toward the hole. For now, I could focus on celebrating our victory with them.

The Fruit of Life was safely tucked away in the Leather Crane Bag.

Dia and Tarte flew into my arms as soon as I rose aboveground. I expected this behavior from Dia, but Tarte was usually too embarrassed. It must have been the side effects of Beastification.

I was relieved to see them both unhurt.

"You were great, my lord," said Tarte.

"Your plan couldn't have been better this time," agreed Dia.

"Everyone played their roles perfectly. This was a team victory," I replied.

If any one of us had failed, the mission would have fallen apart. We truly were the best team.

We hugged to share in the joy that we were all safe, then pulled apart.

Dia squinted at me.

"Something feels off. There's a strange mana around you."

"About that... The Fruit of Life ended up forming. I was exposed to it when I put it away."

Although I'd resisted consuming it, the waves it gave off had still washed over me.

No power had leaked out of the Leather Crane Bag after I put the Fruit of Life into it, but I was worried about the other items inside. I knew putting the fruit in there was a risk, but there was no way I could leave it behind, and carrying it by hand was not an option, either.

"Are you going to be okay?" Dia asked.

"I wasn't exposed for too long. The energy should scatter on its own eventually... I can't have anything happen to you two, though. You should keep your distance from me for a bit. Tarte, take Dia on your hang glider and return home first," I ordered.

Neither one of them moved.

"If anything happens to you, you'll need someone nearby to deal with it. There's no way we can abandon you," insisted Dia.

"I will stay by your side, too. If you say you're okay, my lord, I believe you," Tarte added.

"...Thanks."

We were all in the same boat now. I couldn't call it logical, but I was sure the three of us would get through it just fine.

"Tarte, Dia, step back," I ordered, putting them behind my back to protect them.

By probing the wind, I had detected a presence nearby. Facing it, I drew my concealed gun.

"After insisting on just watching this entire time, now you decide to show yourself...Naoise."

The man before us was my friend who had been manipulated by the snake demon Mina into abandoning his humanity to grow stronger.

Evidently, he'd grown even more powerful since we last met. That surely meant he had gone even farther past the point of no return.

"I wanted to fight, too, but Mistress Mina ordered me not to."

It's Mistress *Mina, is it?*

Last I saw, Naoise and Mina were equals in their relationship. Now he was referring to her as a superior.

She had him wrapped around her finger. At least Naoise still wanted to fight for humankind. He wouldn't have wanted to battle a demon otherwise.

"I see. Let's get to the point. You waited this long to show yourself. I assume you have something to tell us?"

"I want you to follow me. Mistress Mina is waiting for you."

Naoise pointed at the ground, and a giant snake emerged from that spot. He climbed up on top of its head and beckoned for us to join him. The snake was enormous, so there was plenty of room.

"What if I refuse?"

"I would have to fight you."

Naoise drew his magic sword.

Although he was more capable than last time, I would still beat him. Unfortunately, he was strong enough that I couldn't risk holding back, so I'd be forced to kill him.

I thought of Naoise as a friend, so I wanted to avoid that. Plus, I wanted to speak with Mina anyway.

"Got it. Let's go. I've never traveled by snake before… Tarte, Dia, stay close to me."

"Trust me, I will. I hate snakes," said Dia.

Nervously, Tarte remarked, "…This is kind of scary."

They both grabbed on to my collar, and we climbed onto the snake's head together. I expected the scales to be slippery, but the creature's head provided surprisingly solid footing, and it had a number of horns you could grab on to for balance.

Once we were all on, Naoise spoke words that were clearly not in a human language. The serpent responded by taking off at a speed that outpaced a horse-drawn carriage.

Undoubtedly, we were bound for Mina's secret demon hideout. There was no way she would let us ride a giant snake into a town where she operated as a human.

Mina absolutely knew what the earth dragon—that faceless demon—was doing.

Despite that, she'd elected to give me no information. I

wanted to know why. Depending on how this went, my alliance with Mina could collapse.

Should that come to pass, getting out of her den alive would be difficult. I needed to make preparations before we arrived.

I assumed the worst, because that is what assassins do.

Afterword

Thank you very much for reading *The World's Finest Assassin Gets Reincarnated in Another World as an Aristocrat*, Vol. 5.

I'm Rui Tsukiyo, the author.

I'm so glad you chose to read Volume 5.

I bet some readers were surprised by how the goddess acted this time!

The unavoidable return of the Demon King and the hero's terrible blunder are fast approaching. Please look forward to the next book!

Promotion

The second volume of the manga, drawn by Hamao Sumeragi, releases in July. Please check it out!

The anime adaptation of my other series, *Redo of Healer*, also published by Kadokawa Sneaker Bunko, is proceeding smoothly, and its broadcast schedule should be announced soon. (It's a pretty lewd revenge story.)

Not much longer until it airs! Please check that out, too.

Thanks

To Reia, thank you for providing wonderful illustrations for this volume as well.

To Miyagawa, my lead editor, thank you for always giving me such quick and honest responses.

To the editing team; all involved at Kadokawa Sneaker Bunko; lead designer, Takahisa Atsuji; and all the people who have read this far, thank you very much!

The World's Finest Assassin Gets Reincarnated in Another World as an Aristocrat, Vol. 5

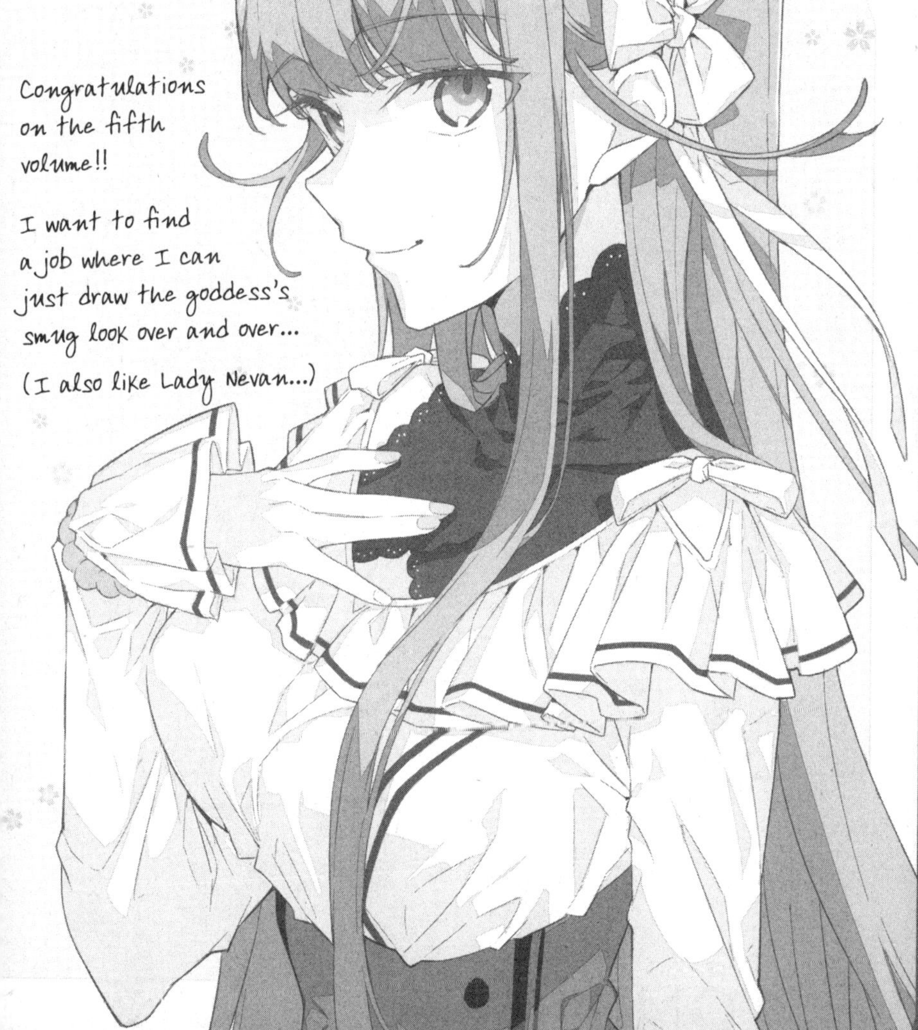

Congratulations on the fifth volume!!
I want to find a job where I can just draw the goddess's smug look over and over...
(I also like Lady Nevan...)

Next Time

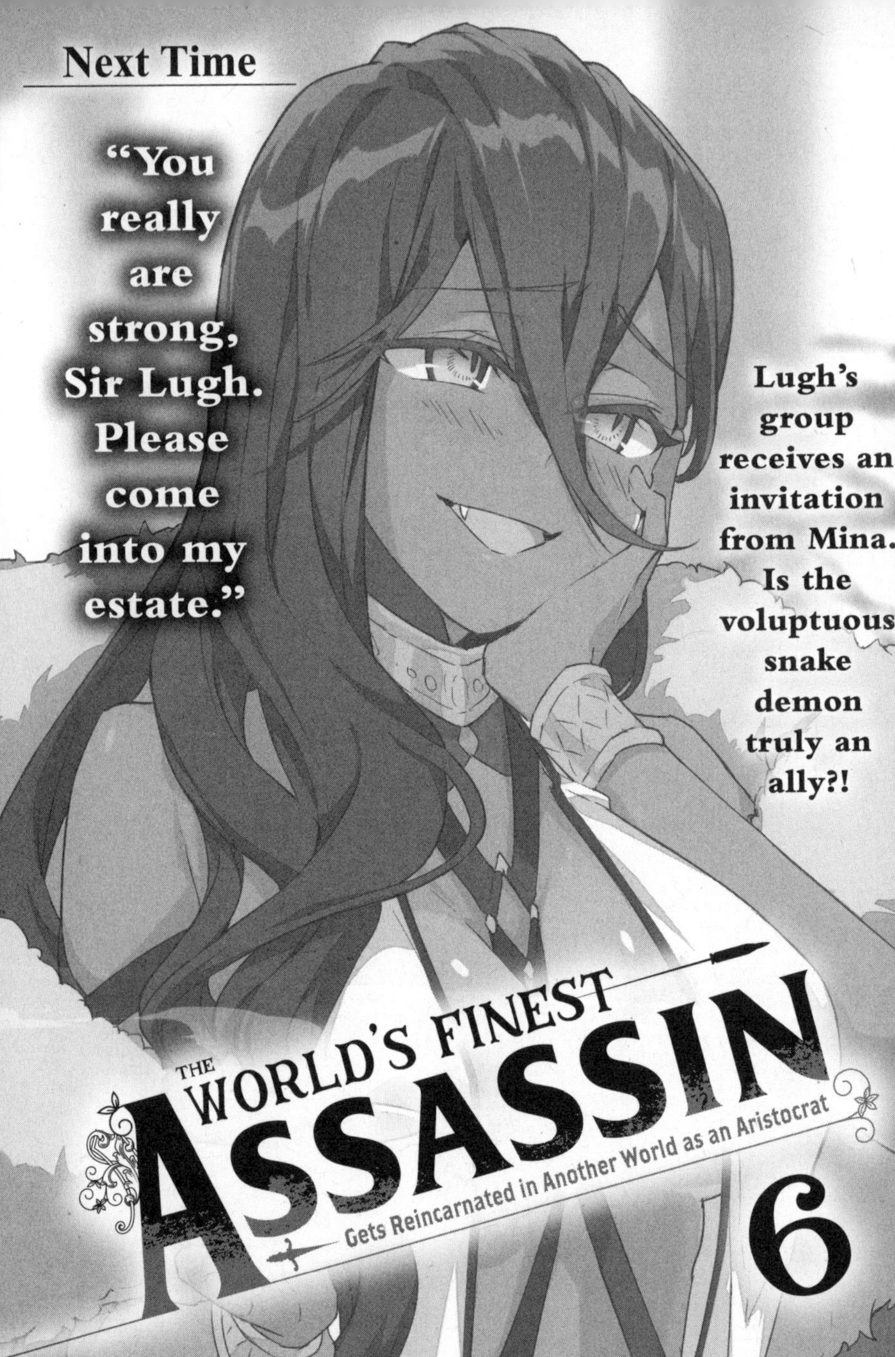

COMING FALL 2022!